Provenance

What people are saying about Provenance*:*

"In clear-eyed, luminous prose, Sue Mell tells the story of a man submerged in grief and impossible yearnings who digs his way out of the remnants of a former life. D.J. scrutinizes his vanishing options with the startling honesty of a man bewildered by circumstance, adrift in his suddenly unrecognizable existence, but always articulate, always a charmer. In this wise and beautiful novel, everyone falls in love with D.J., including the reader."
—Megan Staffel, author of *The Exit Coach*

"Sue Mell's *Provenance* is a relatable, intricate novel about later-life reckoning that (like the antiques store it features) offers up plenty of treasures for the reader."
—Debra Spark, author of *Unknown Caller*

"Ultimately, this is a book about kindness, compassion, and sacrifice—old-fashioned virtues that, Mell shows us, still hold their value."
—Peter Turchi, author of *Maps of the Imagination*

"Sue Mell's searingly beautiful prose and her truly troubled, truly decent characters make *Provenance* a gorgeous, unforgettable novel about learning how to value what is most important in life: those we love and those who show us how to be better."
—Susan Scarf Merrell, author of *Shirley: A Novel*

"Wisdom of great depth and span marks each page of Sue Mell's *Provenance*. The reader intimately experiences the characters making the difficult effort to recognize who they were and who they are, not for the sake of easy absolution, but for the intention of living more authentically."
—Kevin McIlvoy, author of *One Kind Favor*

"Sue Mell's *Provenance* is a novel of irresistibly messy lives, loves, and legacies that, ironically, reads immaculately. Not a letter, not a paragraph, is out of place in this beautiful, beautiful book."
—Liam Callanan, author of *Paris by the Book*

"Packed with exquisite prose, *Provenance* fills the reader with both admiration and anxiety—until the very end, when the main character, who fizzled away his previous life and has come to live in his divorced sister's basement, realizes he might need to rethink his purpose."
—Jane Anne Staw, author of *Small: The Little We Need for Happiness*

"Long after I read the last page, this book sings in my heart."
—Olga Zilberbourg, author of *Like Water & Other Stories*

Provenance

Sue Mell

LAKE DALLAS, TEXAS

FIRST EDITION

Provenance is a work of fiction. Names, characters, places, and incidents either are the products of the author's imagination or are used fictitiously. Any resemblance to actual events, locales, businesses, companies, or persons, living or dead, is entirely coincidental.

Requests for permission to reprint material from this work should be sent to:

Permissions
Madville Publishing
P.O. Box 358
Lake Dallas, TX 75065

Author Photograph: John Bessler
Cover Design: Jacqueline Davis
Cover Art: Sue Mell

ISBN: 978-1-956440-02-7 paperback, 978-1-956440-03-4 ebook
Library of Congress Control Number: 2022932000

For Mary Yntema and Jay Lyons.
Wish you were here for this.

I'm standing in your corridor
I wonder what I'm waiting for
The leaves are drifting out to sea
I'm waiting for you desperately

All things beautiful, all things beautiful
I want everything, I want everything

—Cracker

PROLOGUE

There was so much stuff, piles and piles of stuff, and DJ couldn't let any of it go. Closets and dressers, cabinets and drawers—bookshelves, milk crates, the cedar chest in the hall—all overflowing. A landslide of his jewel-cased CDs, new, used, and traded. Ziggurats of yellow and black Kodak boxes filled with Belinda's prints and negative sleeves. Commercial work—the weddings and portraits she'd begun to do—and the fine art photography she'd always aspired to.

From where he sat, before the monitor of her outdated computer, DJ looked back at their living room, his gaze settling on the trio of cherished items crowning the white-painted chifforobe. A piece they'd found on the street and dragged up the stone stoop and the steep narrow flight to their second floor apartment, delighting more in the word—*Shall I put this in the chifforobe?*—than its ultimate functionality. On the far end was a celadon-glazed tea-pot in the shape of a sage-like, long-mustachioed and -bearded Asian man cuddled by a deer whose tenderly curving neck formed the handle, its head happily resting on the wise man's shoulder. DJ had found it just around the corner at the antiques store on Fourth Avenue, given it to Belinda for their fifth anniversary, along with a set of tiny colored pencils for the traditional wood. The gentle clink of its lid, her soft *Oh* when she peeled back the silvery tissue paper the clerk had used. Why did some things stick while others so easily faded?

Alongside the teapot rested a paper cigar box Belinda had decoupaged with fishing scenes, black-and-white photos she'd clipped from old *National Geographics*, then hand-colored to poignant effect. She'd assembled it when a good cigar box was hard to come by, a time before you could order ten or more from Amazon with a single click, which, to her, made everything less special. For him, the convenience, the instant gratification—and perhaps his indolence—outweighed that loss. Completing this tonal collection, high above the fray, was the surf-green shark ukulele their friend Tracy had given him in honor of his fortieth birthday, back when he owned a mere three or four guitars, when Belinda might fault but still enjoy the benefits of his heedless extravagance, long before her body betrayed them.

In an act of impressive follow-through, Belinda had removed the broken-hinged door of the chifforobe, intending the interior shelves as the fresh space for a curated display of their best finds from flea markets and stoop sales, their favorite *objets d'art*. But the shelves soon filled with stacks of bills and a mishmash of art supplies and guitar pedals, amp cords and unread magazines, film canisters and dirty ashtrays, and whatever else had no place to go. A dust-gathering jumble that blended into the disarray of their lives. *Belinda*. His wife, his love, his own messy girl.

DJ had lived here, in this Park Slope apartment, for thirty years: one alone, twenty-six with Belinda, and then, bereft, for the last three since she'd died. In his grief, he'd thrown himself into a series of relationships, picking up where old flames and unspoken flirtations had left off. All of them with women who'd known Belinda, everyone missing the past, facing a future of limited options. The romances faltered, but the shambles of his once spacious two-and-a-half-bedroom apartment endured, the tide of objects on a continual rise.

A heap of flattened Amazon boxes had grown shoulder-high, filling the so-called half bedroom, lined with floor to ceiling shelves containing his vast, now inaccessible, collection of records. Pop, rock, and country; alternative, classical, and opera; a group he categorized as oddities. Dogs barking Christmas songs. The Leonard Nimoy discography. DJ's turntables, tape deck, and CD player unreachable, replaced by his iPad anyway. There were drugs enough still floating around, amber bottles of liquid morphine, even some Dilaudid, were he a person of that kind of courage. But the odds were much greater of him being pinned by collapsing shelves, buried beneath a cascade of books and half-forgotten tchotchkes, than of him making a deliberate exit.

From the stack of guitar cases depressing the already sunken futon love seat, DJ pulled the Martin for which he'd paid a high price, its sound and beauty irresistible. Tomorrow, along with all but one of his guitars—eight other acoustics, two electric, and one twelve-string, plus the banjo Belinda had wanted to learn to play—the Martin would find its own temporary home in Tracy's recording studio. *Do not bring too much crap,* his younger sister Connie had stipulated as part of her taking him in, when DJ learned that his building had sold, the management's letter brief and final, its plain white envelope slipped under his door. The half-finished basement of the two-bedroom house Connie shared with her eleven-year-old daughter was already crowded, she'd said, with stuff from her own, separation-impelled, downsizing.

To Hurley, DJ would take only the vintage Gibson he'd been playing of late, a suitcase and duffel's worth of clothes, a single yellow Kodak box filled with a mix of mementos and photographs, and the ceramic figurine of a Thai dancer that Belinda had loved. It didn't so much remind him of her as it felt imbued with her affection for the delicate tilt of the dancer's head, the way she balanced on one foot, wrists and elbows flexed, the expression on her porcelain face both impish and sweet.

The rest of their belongings would be trucked the hundred miles upstate to a storage unit on the outskirts of Hurley, the small town where he and his sisters had grown up. Tracy was seeing to that too, arranging for a relay of friends to box and bag everything, whether worthy or not—there wasn't time left for sorting. "I'll pay for the takeout," he'd said, though his resources were slim. He'd quit working when Belinda was dying, blown through the money from her insurance with a determined recklessness. What was left of his life? "You handle the rest," he'd told Tracy. "I don't want to be there." To Connie, a social worker and formidable force, he'd simply said, "Okay."

1

It was not an auspicious beginning. The bus from Port Authority had broken down in Fort Lee. "It's not my fault," DJ said, finally reaching Connie by phone. "Is it ever?" she said, making him think about turning around, except where could he go? Shivering in the cold March air, an old-school accordion folder of his essential papers tucked under his arm, he smoked through his open pack and half the new one wondering what it would be like living under his sister's roof. He should've gotten her a housewarming—a house-mooching—present. For anybody else, he'd buy a gag gift from the 7-Eleven in whose parking lot he and his fellow passengers waited, in varying degrees of impatience, for the replacement bus. But Connie wouldn't be amused, the favor she was doing him too big for anything goofy.

The elastic cord around the folder had long lost its give. One good tip would cast its contents to the winds of New Jersey. Passports present and past; certificates of birth, marriage, and death; all the various IDs he'd accumulated over the years; a half-completed list of passwords Belinda had begun for him at one point; a photocopy of the check from her insurance policy with its stunning sequence of zeros—among other things. A capsule version of his life, minus a few salient details.

Aboard the new bus, DJ slept the rest of the way, and when he got off in Kingston—the first time he'd seen

Connie since Belinda's funeral—she wrapped him in a hug so tight he wished he'd at least bought a 3 Musketeers bar, her childhood favorite.

"It's changed, and it hasn't," Connie said as they bridged the no-man's-land of undeveloped property between Kingston and Hurley.

DJ shielded his eyes, the harsh flicker of sunlight through bare trees making him queasy.

"When did *that* happen?" he said, bracing a little as she took the wide bend around a modern-looking cemetery.

"Are you kidding? That's always been there. They've just added a sidewalk."

"Weird."

"I'll say."

"Connie."

"What?"

"Can we swing by the stone houses?"

"Now? You know I have to get back."

"Sorry. I just thought—"

"It's fine. I can go that way, but I'm not stopping."

"You're the best."

"Blah, blah, blah."

"Connie."

"Did you see that? He just rolls through the stop like I'm not even here."

"Thanks for taking me in."

"Don't thank me till you see the basement. It's hardly Shangri-la."

In the center of Connie's narrow kitchen, a creamy white colonial balustrade lined the open stairwell leading to the basement, each stair creaking as DJ ferried down his bags and the guitar. The space was clean, the floor newly tiled with cork he'd wager she'd installed herself. An oval coffee table sat on a brightly striped Mexican throw rug in front of a worn leather fold-out couch. Connie had put out a pillow, a bath towel, and a set of lavender gingham sheets, along with an old-school sleeping bag, its red flannel lining featuring broncos and cowboys. Everything he could need.

"Looks like Shangri-la to me."

Connie scowled. "I've got regular blankets if you want. The sleeping bag was Elise's idea."

"So, she still remembers me?"

Connie gave a nod to the ping-pong table taking up half the room. "Only one to ever beat her dad. Maybe you guys can play."

Early on in her marriage to David, DJ had helped him retrieve the ping-pong table from their parents' sun porch. Now bankers' boxes were stacked on one end, clear bins of clothing on the other, an empty set of plastic drawers below, hemmed in by U-Haul boxes. Nevertheless, the net was strung, a pair of paddles wedged against it. He'd always liked David, and it took a second to realize she meant with Elise.

"Just the once," he said. "A real Christmas miracle." He hadn't wanted to play, but Belinda insisted—that trip the last she'd made.

"Very merry all around."

Maple shelves lined the long wall, strategically filled with books and games, framed photos, and other keepsakes. Connie tugged at a puzzle, pushed it an infinitesimal amount further in.

"David was high half the time and things were already getting shitty between us."

"But he's not using now."

"No—he isn't."

DJ knew it was not his place, but he couldn't help it. "So?"

"So nothing. Only you live in a fantasy world."

He could hardly deny it. "I thought I was living with you."

"Seriously?"

"I know, I know. But I always thought—"

Connie held up her hand. "So did I. Can we please move on?"

He sat down, patted the arm of the couch. "Was this ... "

"From the den."

DJ slid over. He'd kept nothing from their parents' house. "You wanna sit?"

"I wish. David's picking up Elise from school. They'll be here around three-thirty. I've got a late meeting—a fucking peer review—but I'll be home by seven. These are for you." She handed him a set of keys on a ring with a red plastic tab and a cup-sized, pale pink metal bucket.

"In case I want to make sandcastles?"

"I didn't have an ashtray. And only in the yard—do not smoke in my house."

"How do you know I haven't quit?"

Connie sniffed, wrinkling her nose. "Leopard ... tiger—how's that saying go?"

"I'm sorry I didn't bring you anything."

"Enough, Deej."

"I'll get something for Elise."

"If you must." At the stairs, she turned back. "Help yourself to whatever from the fridge."

"*Go,*" he said. "I'll be fine."

DJ pinged the keys against the little bucket, marking time as he hummed the verse to Gilbert O'Sullivan's "Alone Again (Naturally)." Six weeks at number one in 1972, he found, searching the web on his phone, topped only in US sales by Roberta Flack's "The First Time Ever I Saw Your Face." *Perfect,* he said aloud.

4

He'd forgotten, or Connie had never said, she couldn't spend the afternoon, though there might've been some question of his midweek arrival. No question now except what to do with the rest of the day. She'd barely slowed as they passed the short row of stone houses on Main. Centuries old, they called to DJ with the same fascination they'd held when he was a boy. Not for their historic significance, or the absurd reenactments of colonial life that took place, a single Saturday each July, when they opened to the public. But for the quiet way they stood, with their high-peaked roofs, their wooden shutters, as if they knew him, recognized the skinny kid he'd been, zooming by on his bike, as if they'd said *hello*. He'd tried to explain it once, to Belinda, who'd only smiled indulgently and kissed his cheek.

He was a little turned around when he started walking, but that was what Google Maps was for, the houses as good a place as any to start. Then maybe he'd head right back into Kingston—noodle around the Stockade District, get a bite to eat, something practical for Connie, something not for Elise. The storage space was pushing the limit on his card, but *what the fuck*.

He didn't remember there being a bus, but was glad enough to hop on, cutting the long walk by half. From Kingston Plaza, the next and closest stop, DJ found his way to the old brick Senate House. How many Saturday mornings had their parents dropped him and his sisters off at this touristy landmark, with only a strict pick-up time and the now ironic admonishment that he, the next closest in age, should look after Connie? Their elder sisters, Gretchen and Denise, had a life apart, meeting up with their friends as though unrelated. Spotting them among the canopied shops lining Wall Street, he and Connie would wave wildly, just to get on their nerves. He hadn't minded her tagging along, liked showing her records and his favorite books, poring over candy counters, using his bigger allowance to bolster hers.

When it became clear Belinda was going to die, Denise had driven down one weekend from Rutland, Vermont, picked up Gretchen in Saratoga Springs, and spent the night in Hurley. Then the three of them had driven down to Park Slope, their visit exhausting Belinda, their flood of sympathy and unwanted advice sapping his precious time with his wife, their shock at the disarray of his apartment leaving him furious and unforgiving. What did they know? Connie's general disapproval aside, it was better the few times she came by herself. Then Belinda died. She died. And after the flurry of her funeral, he declined further visits and invitations, could no longer cope with their calls, even his contact with Connie dwindling to none. A year had passed since they'd spoken when he had to ask for her help, a year in which her marriage had fallen apart. Standing before the Senate House, like the stone houses, unchanged, DJ lit a cigarette. His timing had never been good.

DJ wandered into this store and that, the clerks' welcome aggressive in the mid-week slump, though nothing caught his eye. Out of habit, he scanned the window of an antiques shop, the eclectic collection artfully arranged. It wasn't the right place for the gifts he sought, but the sun had faded, the air grown colder, so he stepped inside. Among the tin signs and silhouette portraits, the amateur landscapes and embroidered homilies crowding the wall, a neon-ringed clock with a Coca-Cola logo read twenty past four. He hadn't eaten lunch, didn't know how the afternoon had slipped away.

"Is that the correct time?" he asked the young woman behind the counter, her head down in the penny ads.

She looked up at him blankly, then cocked her head. The frames of her glasses—oval, blue, metallic—caught the light. "Do I know you?"

"I don't see how you could." He'd quit shaving months ago, given free rein to a mustache and beard that came in fully white, making him look not unlike the plump Asian man of the celadon teapot, though nowhere as wise. His own face unrecognizable at times, a stranger glimpsed in passing reflections. The woman, he saw now, wasn't so much young as she had a youthful demeanor, lent in part by a stylish haircut, boyish on one side, the other a more feminine wave of dark hair gracefully framing her face. A weary intelligence placed her closer to his age, certainly within a decade, though she was trim and well-kept in all the places and ways he'd let go. Seated among the antiques, the once treasured belongings of the dead and dispossessed, she had something fluid and vibrant about her that transcended era and style.

She crossed her arms and leaned back in the chair, eyes narrowed, her expression intent as though trying to place him. "No—I've seen you before."

"I just moved back here. Today."

"Then I must be mistaken. But the time," she said, checking her watch against the clock, "is correct. Zero-sum."

"I could buy something," DJ offered.

"You're in luck then. Everything here is for sale. Including that clock, which once belonged to a famous starlet."

He laughed. "This is not your place, is it?"

She opened her mouth, as if to correct him, then shook her head.

"I'd have remembered you," he said, "if we'd met." He should call for a taxi, spend a little time with his niece, but didn't want to return empty handed. He bypassed a wooden crate of records on a nearby table, 78s in their plain brown paper sleeves with cut-out centers, the dark satiny edges of half-inch boxes housing opera and other classical compilations. He surveyed the walls, the various central displays, and though the quality seemed better than average, he saw nothing to capture the interest of an eleven-year-old girl. The smile he gave the woman was meant to convey his apologies: there was nothing for him here.

She shrugged. "It's all junk to me. My brother says people need a story. They want the—"

"Provenance."

"The *provenance*. His wife's four days overdue. Either she's gonna give birth or she's gonna kill someone. So now I'm here, holding down the fort. Let's see…" She braced one hand on the counter top, reached into the top tier of the display case that supported it, and brought out a glass egg paperweight with streaks of white marbled into a dark green. "This came from my grandmother's attic. I'll let you have it for fifteen bucks."

"A much better story. Your brother would be proud."

"I doubt it. That one's actually true. Twelve dollars. He can put it toward the baby's college fund."

DJ picked up the egg, the glass cool and satisfyingly heavy. He said, "I'll give you twenty."

"Now you're taking all the fun out of it."

She reached under the counter again and brought forth a yellow sticky note, which she held out for him to see, the paper stuck to the tips of her first two fingers. Written in red Sharpie, in neat capitals, was the phrase "NOT LESS THAN TEN!!" As she extended her arm, the ribbed cuff of her sweater—steely gray and worried thin at the edge—had pulled away from her wrist, and DJ imagined smoothing his thumb across the pale skin, the ridge of tendons beneath it. "Double exclamation points—that always makes me insane."

"This whole case," she said, sticking the note to the

countertop, "is Alex's idea of point of purchase. That's my brother. The father-to-be. Single-handedly keeping 3M in business. I shouldn't bash him. This place does okay."

"When you're not here?"

She drew her head back. He'd taken it too far. But then she gave him a small twisting smile of concession and DJ felt a warm flood of gratitude spread through his chest and down his arms. The one thing he had left. Over the course of their marriage, Belinda had come to resent the friendships he took up so easily, the women whose interest in her was a secondary, if admiring effect. *Why does everybody love you?* she'd asked him once, and he'd understood she was really asking, *Why don't they love* me? Belinda picking out silver and garnet earrings in a shop much like this one; Belinda bloated and bald in turquoise flannel pajamas patterned with wooly sheep, oxygen tanks rising like silos from the mounting piles of dirty laundry that surrounded their bed. In their last years he'd given her his all, and while he tried to be at peace with that, it hadn't always been the story.

DJ set the egg down on the yellow square. "Let me at least give you the fifteen you asked for."

The woman took a sheet from the *PennySaver* and wrapped the egg. Without looking at him, she wrote up a receipt, carefully detached and slid it toward him. She'd made it out for ten dollars with the words "final sale" written in an elegant script.

"It's a *paperweight,*" she said. "I'll tell my brother you drove a hard bargain."

This was the moment he might've asked her out, or at least asked her name, if she hadn't said, "Anyone who moves back here deserves a break."

He was a fifty-seven-year-old man crashing on the couch in his sister's basement. He picked up the egg in its nest of ads and slid it into his coat pocket. What would

Elise want with a paperweight? He would keep the egg. He let his hand rest on the counter a final time. "Maybe I'll see you around."

"It's a small town," she said, and he turned toward the door.

Outside, a minor bustle of ending shifts heralded evening; waitresses and bank clerks shaking off their dull afternoon to reconvene at the bar up the street. A cocktail would be just the thing, had he someone to share it with. As per Belinda's last wishes, small tins of her ashes had been given to a circle of close friends to disperse as they would, along with a thick vellum card, letter-pressed in pale blue ink, with her secret recipe for the perfect lemon drop. He hugged his coat to his chest, the marbled egg in his pocket banging into his thigh as he hurried against the wind, back to the shelter of Kingston Plaza. For a second time, he found himself smoking in a parking lot waiting on a bus, only what this morning seemed almost a lark, felt more like penitence.

Midway through his marriage, he'd betrayed Belinda. Even in her last years, they'd be walking down a Brooklyn or Manhattan street, and she'd say, "I have that feeling," meaning if they turned right instead of left, they'd run smack into Sarah.

DJ closed his eyes. It was the woman in the antiques store—not so much the way she looked, though that, too, but the way she'd studied him—that reminded him of Sarah. The girl he'd fallen for at nineteen, the best friend of his then girlfriend's younger sister. They'd all been half in love, the way you were at that age, but Sarah … well, Sarah was Sarah. His other true, if thwarted, love.

In their early twenties, one would inevitably be with someone else when the other was free. Once, she visited him at the record store where he was working, near

Bloomingdale's, and he'd given—stolen for her, really—a red heart-shaped record, Bobby Caldwell's sole hit "What You Won't Do for Love." But their affair, a decade or so later, would ruin Sarah's long-standing friendship with Belinda, and ultimately with him, too.

A respectable year after Belinda died, he'd called her, but their attempt to resurrect what they'd each believed to be their alternate destiny had only proved another painful fiasco. At this point, he didn't even know where she was. California, back in New York, or Timbuktu. That Sarah, with whom nothing ever worked out, was alive— and Belinda wasn't—seemed a cruel and ironic twist. How much longer would he have to wait for this bus? Someone had spilled a soda or worse on the bench. DJ took out his phone, saw the battery was dead, and sat down on the yellow curb. A starling landed beside him, its speckled chest strangely vivid in the dimming light. "*Et tu, Brute?*" DJ said, the bird flying off as the bus huffed into the lot.

Still expecting to be home before Connie, DJ felt a little lift at the thought of catching up with David, however soon-to-be-ex he was. The house sat on a small rise, a slate path curved to the front door, and a steep driveway led up to a carport beside the kitchen entrance. Dark pines beyond her property formed a silhouette against the deep, almost glowing, trace of blue left in the sky. Through the living room window, DJ could see Elise seated at the table, head bent to her homework no doubt, beneath the halo of a Tiffany lamp—another remnant from their parents' house. He hadn't thought Connie so sentimental. Or maybe he'd just never noticed these things, more prominent now in a smaller house. Like several of the homes he'd passed, a Moravian star light hung in the carport. After a brief fumble with the keys, DJ came in through the kitchen door to find Connie setting out paper napkins, a large pizza box dominating the table.

"*Oh*," he said. "You're here. What happened to David?"

"What happened to *you?* You don't pick up your phone?"

"Dead battery."

Connie shook her head as though he were an idiot. "I had to reschedule my stupid review and come home," she said, then lowered her voice. "Unlike our parents, I don't leave my kid unattended."

"I was just thinking—wait, what? You said David—"

"Would drop her off. I thought you'd be here."

"You didn't make that clear."

"Apparently. What was so pressing you couldn't spend the afternoon with your niece your first day back?"

"I went into Kingston. To get her a gift."

"Oh, for fuck's sake. Are you shivering?"

"It's cold out."

"You don't have a hat?"

Before he could stop himself, DJ mimicked her tone. "Meh-meh-meh-meh-meh?"

Connie's eyes widened and he cringed, but then she broke into a sputtering laugh.

"Oh, my God—you're such a pain."

"I'm sorry."

"Yeah. You really are."

"Okay—ow."

"What's so funny?" said Elise from the doorway.

"Your old uncle," Connie said. "All-time bane of my existence. Come say hello."

Elise held her hand up, a shoulder-high greeting that DJ matched. Pale blue eyes, wispy fawn-colored hair hanging down to her shoulders—from the window, he'd just seen a girl lost in concentration, but up close she was his little sister at that age, the resemblance so striking he felt time falter, his head grow light.

"We're going to need some ground rules," Connie said. "And I'm going to need you to do something for me tomorrow, but we'll talk about that later. Take your coat off. Sit down, Elise, honey. Let's eat."

DJ draped his coat over the basement rail, the sliding wool bulk of it hanging into the open stairwell against the drag of the paperweight. How well the marbled egg would've tucked in beside the celadon teapot on the wonky chifforobe in his Brooklyn apartment. Should he give it to Elise? To *get* her a gift, he'd said—not that he'd found one. He slid the weighted end of his coat up a little higher, then joined them at the table. He had time to decide.

2

Unable to sleep, DJ watched episodes of *Deadliest Catch* on his iPad until daylight had crept around the staircase. In what felt like minutes after he'd finally drifted off—still dressed, not having opened or made up the couch—Connie sent Elise down with a cup of coffee. What she needed him to do was come with her when she dropped Elise at school, then drive over to her old house, where they were headed now, so DJ could take David's car and use that to fetch Elise after school. For the time being, she explained, David was living there, tasked with finishing the repairs that, in a terrible market, would bring them the best possible price and—having reached the end of the year's separation required by New York state—enable them to more formally divide their assets and finalize their divorce. David's work as a contractor had slowed—she wasn't so flush herself. But he was meeting with a potential client and, since DJ was here, she saw no reason to take the afternoon off.

"No problem," said DJ, though the last car he'd driven was a rented Fiat. Northern Italy, Paris, and the south of France—a two-week trip, blown for in the reckless joy of Belinda's brief remission. Five years. How long ago and far away that seemed; how impossibly optimistic he'd been.

"The pick-up line's long—you'll want to get there early."

"Early," he said. "I got it." It had spooked him to see Elise file into the crowd of kids, her hand raised in a backhanded wave for her mother's sake, all the terrible years of middle school still to come her way.

"And don't talk about me with David. Not that he'll think to ask, but if he does. I know you two were always yukking it up at the holidays."

"No we weren't," DJ said, but he knew what she meant.

"Open the glove box, will you? My sunglasses are in there." She lowered her window and inhaled deeply. "Smells like spring."

Connie worked at the state hospital. The kind of crushing, impossible job few people can stand up to day after day, year after year, without giving up hope. Teens who tried to kill themselves, their parents, each other. DJ passed her the glasses and she slipped them on, a pair of Ray-Bans that gave her a glamorous air. She'd been a reckless kid, more of a worry to their parents than he'd ever been. He wanted to ask what had changed, why she and David couldn't work things out. But she bent her head to the wind and he could feel her pure pleasure in driving, marveled at her determination to plunge into the problems of the world, himself included. This was who she'd become.

"What?" she said. "You don't like these?"

"You look great."

"I look like shit, but thanks for saying." She pulled up behind David's truck and honked twice. "I'm just going to wait until he comes to the door."

"I could've rung the bell."

Connie looked past him toward the house, bigger and shabbier than he remembered.

"Shoulda, coulda, woulda," she said.

As he got out of the car, David stepped onto the porch, raised his hand in a single wave. DJ looked back at Connie, who did the same, then drove off. They were the waviest family he'd ever seen.

"So here you are," David said, as DJ came up the steps to meet him. "Returned from the great metropolis. Quite the beard you got going there—you doing all right?"

"I've been better. You?"

"I heard your place was a wreck."

"I heard yours was."

David snorted. "You got any plans?"

"Will there be more insinuations, or can I just have the keys?"

"Today, Deej. I just meant today."

Once he had the car, DJ thought he might give the antiques store another shot. "Just picking up Elise. Maybe a little more sleep."

"I've been reading this book—"

"*Really.*"

"You and Connie—I read. *A River Runs Through It.* You know that book?"

"I know that story."

"Anyway. It made me think about fishing. That I'd like to go. It's a gorgeous day. What do you say?"

"You know the brother dies, right?"

"Not from fishing."

"I thought you're meeting a client."

"Not till this afternoon," David said. "I have to pick something up—but that's on the way. I've got waders in the truck."

"Seriously?"

"No. But I do have a pair of cheap poles and a loaf of white bread. You can fish off the dock at Rondout Creek now."

"I don't know about fishing, but the creek—that is nice. I haven't been to the Rondout—"

"It's not about the fucking fishing, okay?"

The porch had sagged from the house and DJ could feel the give of rotting floorboards as he shifted his weight. "Maybe I should just get the keys."

Lifting one shoulder, David wiped his nose with his T-shirt sleeve. "Sorry. I'm under a lot of pressure. I just thought we'd hang out."

Cowboy good looks, Belinda once said of his prominent jaw, the dimpled chin. David's neck had thickened; his dark curls, skillfully tousled with product, had thinned. But it was the carpenter's pencil tucked behind his ear that pinched DJ's heart, tugged at his allegiances. David was a can-do guy, funny and caring in his own stubborn way, however far he'd fallen short lately—which seemed like it might be a lot.

"She's my sister—it's not that I wouldn't—"

"I know, I know. How's she doing, anyway? All she'll talk to me is logistics."

"She's all right."

"Look. There's this guy—it's a long story. But he owes me money for a kitchen I did last year. He's already bounced one check, says he's got the cash now. Only he's kind of a prick, and I'd just feel better if I had someone with me, even if he does look like Santa Claus."

"This is how you ask for a favor?"

"You're the one taking my car."

"To pick up your daughter."

"One hour. It'll be fun."

"Fine," said DJ. Connie wouldn't have to know. "Long as we stop someplace for cigarettes."

"You're still smoking? Wow."

"It's not like my quitting's going to bring her back."

"Sorry," David said. "I'm a dick. Let me just grab my jacket."

Once again, DJ found himself in the Stockade District, but only passing through, the shops and well-tended homes giving way, after they turned onto Broadway, to a stretch of economic desolation marked by methadone clinics and hot dog joints.

David pulled into a Sunoco station. "Winstons, right?"

"Soft pack," DJ said, but David returned with a carton. "You didn't have to do that."

"Can't be easy, coming back."

"Hasn't been long enough to say."

"Right, right."

They drove on a little farther, then David turned down a series of one-way streets, the houses more and more run-down, old tires and broken swings in the yards, people sitting on their porches like it was a full-time job. The one they pulled up in front of had a widow's walk and a distinctive lean.

"This house," DJ said. "You did a kitchen in this house."

"Don't be stupid. His wife's got a place in Saugerties, but she kicked Skip out."

"Skip."

"It's a name."

"You're a terrible liar."

"That may be so, but this is where he's staying. Or he was."

Someone peeked out, pulling aside the eyelet fabric covering the glass on the door.

David turned off the engine, glanced up and down the block. "Maybe you should stay in the truck."

"I thought the whole point—"

"I know what I said. Now I'm saying something else."

DJ looked back at the house. A sandy-haired man wearing an REO Speedwagon T-shirt and cut-off sweats was carefully making his way down the porch steps in bare feet, a folded newspaper in his hand. Sporting a deep tan, he looked like an aging surfer.

"Is that *Skip?*"

"Can you please just shut up?"

The man held up his hand and continued walking gingerly down to the curb. David got out of the truck, slammed the door behind him. "*Ryan*," he said, "What the fuck?"

Ryan put a finger to his lips, nodded toward the house. "Patrice is here with my daughter." He, too, glanced up and down the street, then handed David the paper. "Half is all I've got."

"This is not right." David took the paper, tucked it under his arm. "You tell Skip ... "

Ryan waited, his chin raised, as though poised to memorize whatever message there was, but David only pressed two fingers to the space between his brows and shut his eyes. Then he opened them and looked directly at DJ. "Oh, what's the point." To Ryan he said, "Just tell him I'm done."

David got in the truck, thumped his head on the steering wheel, then let it rest there.

DJ waited until Ryan had heel-toed his way back to the house. "You want to tell me what that was?"

"I do not."

I can see, DJ was tempted to say, how this kind of thing might make trouble in a marriage. "You mind if I smoke?"

"Do whatever you want."

"Oh, *now*," DJ said drawing out the word. He opened the carton, tapped a pack on the dashboard, his fingers shaking only a little more than usual.

David lifted his head, pulled a business-size envelope from the folded paper, slipped it into the inside pocket of his jacket, and tossed the paper aside.

"Let's just go down to the river. Can you do that for me?"

"You really asking? Or is this just another *courtesy*?"

"*C'mon*," David said. "It's not what it looks like."

"Like I'd know what that is." DJ lit up, exhaled a stream of smoke out into the street. "Except for not good—I understood that part."

"It must get old, always being so clever."

"Old is not the half of it, my friend."

David drove on toward the Rondout and DJ didn't object. Besieged. That was how he felt. But also alive, the plodding rhythm of his last few years jarred into a fresh if unsteady beat. Adrenaline, mostly. Though catching a whiff of the Hudson on the breeze, the morning's chill burning off in the brilliant sunlight, he couldn't help feeling a certain joy, a hooky-playing sense of possibility. This afternoon he'd be on duty with Elise, and come evening, he'd have to tell Connie something about David—whatever that would be. Obligations that were like radio static in the life he'd imagined for himself in Hurley. Quiet. Solitary. Agenda-free. DJ glanced back, and there they were: two fishing poles, rattling against the metal truck bed. Other than raising the dead, he could think of nothing better.

A few blocks before the river, David parked by a small café. Above its gray-painted Dutch door, a transom and clerestory windows, the interior walls stripped to the original brick. More gentrified Brooklyn than upstate New York. DJ would've liked to stop, but David strode on, his gaze trained ahead, the poles in one hand, a loaf of Wonder Bread clutched in the other. In the truck, he'd kept wiping at his nose, his mouth; his jaw continually working as the silence between them grew. Over and over, David shook his head. A twitch-like motion, like he was rejecting things said or one bad idea after another, making DJ wonder—as if an envelope of cash from sketchy Ryan wasn't enough—what else was going on. At the promenade, David paused for him to catch up.

"C'mon, old man."

"Fuck off," DJ said, relieved to take up their habitual jocularity. But after they'd settled on the dock, lines dangling, Jesus bugs skimming the water, whatever reserve David had mustered collapsed.

"I'm in a bit of trouble, Deej."

DJ looked down the wide creek, the line of more serious fishermen staggered along the rail making him think of Belinda's decoupaged box. There'd been a series of them, though she'd destroyed the first two. *Not good enough,* she'd said, but DJ knew it was because she'd assembled them one afternoon with Sarah. Belinda loved the word *palimpsest,* and were she with him, he'd have whispered it in her ear. Instead, he turned back to David.

"I get that."

"Not those guys," he said with derision. "I'm behind on the mortgage. We could lose the house."

"*We?*"

"Don't be smug. And you can't tell Connie."

"Don't do that."

"I don't suppose you have any money."

Before DJ could think what to say, David let out a sharp syllable of laughter. "You should see your face. Like I'd ask you for money."

"You just did."

"A *joke,*" he said, but DJ didn't think so.

"Do you even have a meeting this afternoon?"

"Of course I do. And if things go well, I should get a deposit, but it won't be enough. It might've been, if Skip hadn't fucked me."

"And that envelope?"

David reeled in his line, added a chunk of bread, and cast it out. "Yeah. Most of that belongs to someone else."

DJ set down his pole. "What are you, Scarface now?"

"That doesn't even make sense."

"Why bring me along? Why tell me any of this?"

"I don't know. Because we used to be friends? Because I thought you—of all people—would get it? My brother used to take me fishing at this crappy little pond. There probably weren't even any fish in there, but I loved it anyway. Don't you ever just feel like you want to go back?"

All DJ could do was nod. "Every single day."

21

3

It had taken them three days to pack up his apartment. Three days in which DJ took long last walks, lingered over cups of good coffee in his favorite cafés, or holed up in the bedroom with his headphones on, as they worked, room by room, beginning with the kitchen at the opposite end. This way, Tracy said, he'd have a better sense of things, though the categories would overlap. It was like arranging records by era or emotional ties, rather than alphabetically. Each evening, he'd be amazed at the labeled boxes, the furniture, such as it was, gathered end to end, the empty space around them disturbing. A scouring of memory, a gutting of his life. Gauging by the line of Hefty bags at the curb, half of what filled his apartment had been garbage.

Most of those who came to help were people he hardly saw anymore, old friends whose paths no longer aligned with his—whatever that was. People from what he thought of as the old days, whose eagerness to help him "make a fresh start" only left him more depressed. Freshness was overrated. And in their place, asked to do the same, he'd have said, *Yeah—no thanks.*

All those boxes, all those pieces of his life, were now just a few miles from where he sat in David's car—a silver Camry whose better days had seen better days—waiting to pick up his niece. In a month, maybe less, the little cash he had left would run out, his credit cross the line of his limit. What then would he do with that truckload of stuff? He sure as hell couldn't bring it to Connie's. And how much would he tell her of the morning's absurd escapade? Nothing—according to David. But he had to say something—that much was clear.

After his dockside revelation, David insisted on buying him coffee to "smooth things over"—as if a cup of coffee would make things right. They'd stopped into that little café, the only customers. Seated among those farmhouse tables and chairs, everything sleekly refinished, from the frame of a towering blackboard menu to the maple floor, all DJ could think was how much he missed his life, even the one after Belinda; his desire to be back in Brooklyn a physical pain, his sternum aching as though it were bruised.

An industrial chandelier of pendant bulbs hung above the counter, light glinting off glass-domed stands filled with inviting desserts, and DJ ordered himself a big fat piece of chocolate cake. Then, as if to compound his self-indulgent misery, the woman from the antiques store walked in with an expansive "Hey!" not for him but for David, whose legitimate work included putting in her brother's second bathroom. Connie wanted to put a bathroom in the basement—only she couldn't afford to make improvements on her new house till the old one was sold. David assured him that he'd get the money, that he'd just had a moment, that he'd figure it out— he always had. And DJ wanted to believe him, easily would've until today.

"My brother-in-law," David said, omitting his soon-to-be-ex status as well as DJ's name.

"How funny," she said. "We've met. Nice breakfast," she added, noting DJ's cake.

"We've had a bit of a morning," David said. "You want to sit?"

"Can't. I'm just heading over." The smile she gave DJ was polite. "Nice to see you again."

"DJ," he said.

"Andrea."

"It looks good, by the way." David nodded toward the counter. "She made that chandelier."

"And he helped me hang it."

Did he now, DJ wanted to say. Instead, he said, "You're an artist."

"Hardly."

"It makes the place."

"The cake makes the place, but thanks. I gotta run."

"*It makes the place?*" David said, after she was out of earshot. "Nice try, cake-for-breakfast man."

Though he wished he had it now, he'd pushed his cake aside. Spurred on by humiliation, by whatever danger David had or hadn't put him in, DJ put the question to him.

"How much?"

"How much what?"

"For the house. How much do you need?"

"I told you that was a joke. I wouldn't take it from you."

"Tell me anyway."

"Five. Maybe six hundred dollars."

It wasn't so much. DJ still had his record collection. The hundreds of albums and CDs he'd repeatedly promised Belinda he'd sell. Not for the money, though they could've used it, but for the space. So she could have the darkroom she'd always wanted. He hadn't sold them for her, hadn't sold them at Tracy's behest, when she was packing up his place, but he could sell them now—not for David, but for Connie.

There were some prized releases, the bulk worth a couple hundred at least. More, if he'd kept them in better condition. But that too had gone the way of all things. Just to catalogue them was a lot of work, but there were always dealers who didn't care, who'd buy up the lot for a low-ball price. A last, likely inevitable, resort. Maybe he wouldn't even tell Connie—it could just be the good thing he'd done. Selling them off, getting the money to David, saving what she had no idea she'd come close to losing. That was the fantasy he was lost in when Elise tapped on the glass, opened the passenger door, and tossed her knapsack onto the back seat.

"She didn't tell you to get here early?"

"She did. I just got ... delayed."

Elise got in, yanked the door closed with a slam.

"Whoa. Everything okay?"

"What? Oh. No, you have to slam it, or it doesn't close right."

"Like so many things," DJ said.

They had to wait for the cars ahead to pull out one by one, what flow there was interrupted by groups of kids crossing to the bright yellow buses.

"Did you know it was one guy who determined that all school buses should be that color? A professor at Teachers College. Frank W. Cyr."

The look she gave him was unimpressed.

"You can Google it."

"Is that what you just did?"

"Passes the time," he said, though he'd actually known that one.

"You don't have to entertain me."

"I wasn't—I mean, I was, but not because I have to. Here we go."

Suddenly nervous with Elise in the car, DJ looked back, then checked the mirror twice before he pulled into the through street. And still, the instant he turned, a carful of hooting teenagers came swerving past. Before he left for college, he'd taken Connie to Price Chopper in their parents' car, let her do doughnuts in the parking lot. She'd whooped and hollered like that. A shred of joy to counter the pain of her saying she wished he didn't have to go. Default or defeat, here he was, back in Hurley, just trying to get through the day without getting killed.

25

"What things," said Elise.

"What?"

"What other things do you have to slam?"

"Lockers. My head against the wall. You feel like going somewhere?"

"Not really."

"That's all right," he said, though he was taken aback. "We don't really know each other, do we."

Her eyes met his in the rearview mirror. "Where would you go, if I'd said yes?"

"Aah, now that's a good question." At the next light he could turn toward Connie's or back into Kingston. They could even loop up to the Hudson Valley Mall. "Where would you like to go?"

She made a sound like a buzzer.

"Okay—fine—lemme think." Where he wanted to go was the small used record store he'd bypassed in Kingston. Yesterday, it meant an old habit he'd learned to ignore, almost an itch in his fingers, to flip through display bins of albums, the rare cuts protected in plastic sleeves. He wanted to see what prices were like up here, whether the owner might be interested in what he had or know of a local dealer. Not much fun for Elise, but maybe she'd tolerate it if they went somewhere she wanted first. "I could always go for soft serve."

She buzzed again.

He puzzled for a moment, then the shelves in Connie's basement rose in his mind and he knew he had it. "Bookstore."

"Ding, ding, ding."

"Do the right thing."

"What?"

Her smile, so much like Connie's, dissolved, and along with it the sliver of happiness that, for one brief second, had slid into his heart. "It's just something we used to say."

"You and … Belinda?" she said, as though formulating a complicated equation.

"And a few of our friends." He'd seen this before, with Belinda's nephews, the way a kid could pierce your skin, climb right into your head and all its weaknesses.

Just at the height of his promise, the moment he thought he could break the world apart, a blood vessel had burst in his brain. The defect lying in diabolical wait till he turned twenty-four, then delivering a fate of loss and dependence he'd never rise above. *Ding, ding, ding. Do the right thing.* The aneurysm. He hardly thought about it anymore. He'd been dating Belinda, but was going to leave her, make a real bid for Sarah, take a stake in his future. He'd written music reviews in college, intended to write more for *The Village Voice*, give Greil Marcus a run for his money. Instead it was Belinda who took a leap forward, moving into his Park Slope apartment during his recovery, and sticking it out, through the years-long funk that followed, with a love he couldn't possibly match.

After the aneurysm, well ... it was what it was. Memory returned, but that vivid sense of promise—of what he might accomplish or become—never would. At twenty-four, he'd stepped forward and his brain had blown up. End of story. Only with Sarah had he ever felt anything close, and that hadn't turned out well either. He'd made what he'd made, been whatever he'd been, his marriage the central creation of his life, the significant factor. That, and a little bit of music. *Ding, ding, ding. Do the right thing.* The once-comic refrain of a long-faded era.

Elise repeated the two phrases slowly, as though trying them on. "I still don't get it."

"Yeah," he said, taking the turn into Kingston. "Neither do I."

They went into the used bookstore on Front Street, where a rain of paperbacks dangled from knotted ropes in the window display, and then, at Elise's suggestion, over to

Rhino Records, which hadn't been there when he was a kid, but stocked a carefully curated selection of books, including first editions, along with records, CDs, and a little art.

Elise perused the small selection of zines and graphic novels while DJ spoke with the clerk. He might sell a few things here, but they'd want their markup, too—he might not get the best price. *Good luck to you, man,* the clerk said, giving him a card with the owner's number, and making him feel like some old codger. Only then did DJ notice Elise at his side, listening in.

"My mom has a box of records. The little ones."

"45s," the clerk said, and she shot him a look. "My bad, my bad. Carry on."

"Down in the basement. No record player though."

"Ah," said DJ. "Find anything here you want?"

She shook her head. "You know I have homework, right?"

"Oh, shit—what time is it? Nothing at all? My treat."

"No," she said. "No. I'm all right."

"Well okay, then. *Vámonos.*"

"Thanks, though. Thanks for bringing me."

DJ tried to think of himself at her age. He'd had his head in a book, that's for sure—surrounded by his sisters' chatter. Eleven was moody for anyone, but how lame did you have to be to not give a kid a snack? He'd pick something up on the way back, whatever she wanted, and when they got back to Connie's, he'd give her the glass egg. She was quirky and observant, he got that much now, and he thought she'd like it.

After much deliberation, Elise had chosen a box of Entenmann's cookies and DJ served them up, along with tall glasses of cold milk, on an old transferware plate with a country scene—Connie liked certain vintage things, too. From the basement, he retrieved the egg in its nest of paper and, to his delight, the Platter-Pak his little sister had toted around. A bit grimy and scuffed, but mostly well-preserved, her small suitcase of 45s was white with a pink top, and featured a graphic of a light blue record whose spin lines wove into a musical staff, a treble clef and quarter notes strewn across it, along with a sprinkling of dots and stars. Still filled, he assumed, with singles by The Beatles, The Monkees, and The Dave Clark Five. Records she'd saved for, and a few he'd given her, including Connie's prize—her favorite of favorites—Lulu singing "To Sir with Love." What had been on the flip side? "Let's Pretend."

"First this," he said, presenting his gift to Elise, "then your homework so your mom doesn't have my head."

"It's heavy. What is it?"

"Just open it. I'll keep it if you don't like it, get you something else."

"It's ... swirly." She held it up to the light. "It's beautiful. So green."

"It's meant to be a paperweight. Remnant of a bygone age, when people wrote letters on fine stationery with fountain pens. A collectible now." This wasn't especially true, although it could be; he just wanted to assign it a history, something to imagine when she held it in her hand, to give it more value than the ten dollars he'd paid. A better story than collecting dust in some grandmother's attic.

"I can put it on my windowsill. It'll catch the sun."

DJ thought of the line of amber bottles atop Belinda's bedside bookshelf, the way the morning light through the Venetian blinds would set them aglow. He thought of Andrea beneath that giant clock with its neon ring, how her running into him with David had quashed his hopes of something more. Still, he had the desire to see her, to tell her of the gift's success, which had its own good currency.

"You break out your books. I'm gonna see what your mom's got here in the box."

How many hours had he and Connie spent listening to records in his room? The original cave of music and books—his provenance. Practicality be damned. Using his phone, DJ scrolled and clicked around on Amazon until he found a portable record player that matched the picture in his head. Styled like a briefcase with a white Bakelite handle, the corners reinforced with shiny nickel plate, its sides a retro turquoise that would perfectly match the whirling graphic of musical notes on her record case. Only forty bucks. He knew it wouldn't offset the realities, wouldn't stop whatever trouble David was sending her way. He wasn't a fool; he was just a brother, an uncle, a man with little recourse and an exceptional talent for avoidance. Maybe David would come up with the money. Maybe DJ would help. Either way, it would be a good present, an affectionate gesture, to revive those old songs, bring the music they'd once shared back into her life, pass them on to her girl. It would be what he could do.

DJ drifted down to the basement, where he lay on the couch, the room lit only by the glow of his iPad, as he wrestled with the melody that wouldn't leave him alone. Little more than a loop of phrases, it rolled through a series of shifts, without the fullness he craved or any satisfying resolution. Minor, diminished, augmented—unprepossessing words that belied their potential, was the thought running through his mind when, beyond his headphones, he heard Connie sternly calling his name. One note over and everything changed.

"What's all this?" she said the minute he reached the top of the stairs. Through the living room doorway he caught sight of Elise, the look she flashed him a comedic *yikes*. He turned toward the mess they'd left on the kitchen table: crumpled napkins, dirty glasses, and stacks of 45s, the milk still out, cookies going stale on the plate. "Entenmanns?"

"Hey, mom," Elise called, and DJ was touched by her vain attempt to save him.

"Hey, honey—just give me a sec." Connie set down her bag of groceries and yanked off her coat. "You cannot do this. You've been here five minutes—"

"I won't. It's nothing. I got it." He pulled out a chair. "Have a seat. Have a cookie. Take a load off."

"*Take a load off?* I'm gonna say hello to my daughter, and when I come back, all of this..." She passed her hand over the table, a magician's preparation before the *voilà*. "I got pork chops. Good thick ones, on the bone. Maybe you want to put those in the fridge, too."

His second day back and he could not stay out of trouble.

"You want me to cook?" he asked, catching her off guard. For himself, he'd resorted to take-out and delivery, but during his marriage he'd been the one to cook, for both the pleasure and pure unlikeliness of the endeavor, working his way through *Cooking with Craig Claiborne and Pierre Franey* in the days before the Food Network. He'd liked shopping at the small specialty stores, and later at the enormous Fairway that opened in Red Hook, the surfaces of their cramped kitchen filling with small appliances. Blender, Cuisinart, pasta and waffle makers.

"*No*," said Connie, then her expression softened. "Okay—yeah. That'd be nice. What'd David say about the car?"

DJ picked up the container of milk and turned toward the fridge. *Maybe I'll sell this piece of shit,* was what David had said, finally handing over the keys. "What do you mean?"

"About getting it back."

"Didn't say."

31

"Well, he's gonna have to work that one out with you. I've got enough to worry about."

Now was the time to say something. The longer DJ waited the worse it would get. He didn't want to lie—what could he even come up with? He just didn't want to tell her how he knew what he knew.

After dinner, after she'd tucked in Elise, after one and then a second cigarette in the yard, DJ emptied the little pink bucket and sat Connie down in the living room.

"Well, that can't be right," she said. "He'd have to be months behind. You sure he wasn't pulling your leg? He always thought you were a bit of a sap."

This surprised him, though he certainly felt like one now. He ran the morning's scenarios through his head. Ryan's envelope, the whole I-just-wanna-go-fishing conceit. To be a contractor was to be a hustler of sorts, but David was no master scammer. DJ told Connie only the key points: that David wanted him to go with him to see a client who owed him money, that he said he'd fallen behind, that the house was in jeopardy. To give her the full account of his lapse in loyalty would be needlessly hurtful and mortifying. "It's what he told me. He said that he could—that he would—get the money. I just thought you should know."

"But you didn't think you should call me, didn't think you should tell me when I could still—you know—call the bank."

It hadn't occurred to him, the obvious thing, but what was the point of saying that now?

"I'm just gonna call him." She got her phone and punched in the number, but David didn't pick up, didn't respond when she texted either. Connie looked at him, her eyes full of sudden knowledge. *"What client?"*

DJ hesitated. It would all come out. He'd need to sell his records, maybe even the guitars, just to keep himself off the street.

"Some guy named Skip?"

"No, no," she said, and then a string of no's, over and over.

"Connie."

"You went with him, didn't you? To Saugerties? A month ago, he took a fucking pee test—his idea, because I said he looked ragged. How stupid am I? Like that was even his pee."

Because she'd told him David wasn't using, because he needed it to be true, DJ had written off the signs. Weren't there any number of possible shady things? "I did go with him, but not to Saugerties. Some seedy house in Kingston, but Skip wasn't there. Just some guy with a tan who gave him..." Connie waited. DJ was loath to say it. "An envelope of cash."

"*Ryan*," she said. "That piece of shit. His family owns a salon. All-around bad egg and crony of David's, going back to junior high. You didn't think that was strange?"

"How tan he was?" DJ hung his head. It was like a tic, an uncontrollable impulse—this reflex to crack wise. However sharp, however well-timed the quip, it only made things worse, ninety percent of the time. But the other ten—those perfect moments of hilarity when the tension broke—felt like something he couldn't live without.

"What is wrong with you?"

"I don't know—this is not my..."

"What."

"This is not my world."

Connie pressed two fingers to the space between her brows, the same gesture David had made.

"So, it's good, in a way," he ventured, breaking the silence that now deadened the room, "that at least you know?"

Connie waved him off. "You need to go away from me now, before I say something I'll regret."

DJ sat downstairs on the fold-out sofa, Connie above. He felt bad, the pork sitting like a rock in his stomach, but he was also pissed off. He wasn't the one with a coke habit, the one who'd relapsed—if that was even what David had done. Why should any of this fall on him? This is what happened when you let people help you. You owed and you could never pay back. He may not have done it the way she wanted, but hadn't he done the part that should count? Picked up Elise, spent some time with her, so Connie could go on with her afternoon, taking care of a bunch of people more fucked up than he was. Was it his fault that she wouldn't let Elise take the goddamn bus? His bags were still packed. He could call Tracy, ask to stay with her till he figured something out. Except he couldn't. Not after she'd boxed and bagged up his life, tending to every detail—she'd been the one to suggest he reach out to Connie, maybe settle upstate. It seemed a good enough option at the time. How could he tell her it wasn't? That everything she'd done was for naught?

Tracy was like a thread that had been stitched through his life, the one mutual friend of his college girlfriend to stick beyond that crushing breakup. The first to champion and then love Belinda almost as much as he did. Half of what she'd done for him these past few years an expression of loyalty—not only to him—and a barricade against her own grief. He wouldn't have made it through those first terrible weeks without her—Tracy the person who best knew them both. He'd have married her if he could.

DJ didn't know how long he'd been sitting there before Connie came down.

She cleared her throat. "This isn't what you thought it would be, is it?"

He glanced over to where she stood, one hip resting against the ping-pong table, then returned his gaze to the long stretch of shelves, all the things she'd held onto.

"Nope."

"Not how I pictured it either."

"I'm sure."

"It's only been two days—just because my husband's the fuckup of all time, doesn't mean you and I can't sort things out."

"That's very social-work-y of you."

"C'mon, DJ. I'm trying here."

"I know."

"And I need you to think—just a little bit—and be on my side."

DJ turned so that he faced her directly. "What are you gonna do?"

"That's the question, isn't it? Stop at the bank first thing. Hope he's got the money or at least the decency to call me. You're going to have to drive me, then take my car. I don't want you mixed up in whatever mess he's in. And I sure as hell don't want him driving Elise. I thought…" She ran her hands into her hair and held onto her head—a gesture he must've seen her make a thousand times as a kid. Then she let them drop and looked down at the floor. For a second, he thought she might cry, but she shook her head, a rueful smile fading just as quickly as it had appeared. "He got me a good deal on the cork tile, helped me install it. Told me work had been slow, but was trickling in."

She looked up at him then, and DJ felt the sting of tears. What good was he to her, his little sister? What good was he to anyone?

"I still can't believe that he'd risk the house," Connie went on. "It's so ironic—I'm the caseworker, right? Maybe I just didn't want to see it."

She walked over to the shelves, ran her hand along the

tattered spines of a section of children's books. "So much stuff. What were you doing with my Platter-Pak?"

"Nothing, really." Over dinner, Elise had recounted their trip. "At Rhino Records, I was talking with the clerk and Elise told me you still had all those 45s."

"You wouldn't think there'd be much for her there, but she loves that place." Connie picked up a small ceramic vase, blew on it as though there were dust, though the basement was immaculate, or had been until he arrived, the dregs of his morning's coffee still in a mug on the table, yesterday's clothes on the floor underneath, the sleeping bag a rumpled pile.

"I was thinking of selling my records."

"Aww," she said, with a childlike resistance. "Don't do that."

"It's not like I play them."

"I know. It's just … some things … " She shoved the sleeping bag aside, plunked down beside him. "Do you remember when the best thing in the world to do was hang out and listen to records?"

"I do." DJ remembered Union Square, before the Farmer's Market that distinguished it now, when you walked around instead of through the park to avoid being mugged or knifed. He remembered the walk down to East 12th, the green awning of Academy Records, the quiet comfort he'd felt there. Remembered the day a doppelganger of his eighteen-year-old self had appeared. Long stringy hair falling into a pale face, thrift store peacoat unbuttoned despite the day's chill. Remembered how his spirit had risen in camaraderie as the boy gave him an acknowledging nod across the bins of records. The instant his draw to that place, so sharply etched, became forever diminished. He'd been young there once. He no longer was.

Connie slid down on the cushions, let her head fall back, a picture of exhaustion that twisted his heart. Even the right things he wanted to do were wrong.

"Those seconds before the first track," she said, "waiting for the piano or guitar? Knowing every turn of the music that lies ahead. The pleasure of your favorite song, even the one you wished had been left off the album inseparable from the arc of sheer satisfaction."

DJ smiled to himself—he'd got her a good present, if nothing else. She had her 45s. Maybe he'd hold on to a few records, too.

"It's just a shame."

"Yeah," he said, though he wasn't sure if she meant the records or David—or just the relentless onslaught of time.

4

DJ woke before his alarm, startled into the quiet of his sister's basement, the rise and fall of her footsteps as she moved about upstairs. He couldn't remember what it was he'd dreamed, but the feeling of being back in his apartment clung to his senses, as if Connie's house were the dream he had yet to wake from.

Despite what he'd lost, all he'd squandered and put out of his mind, he still hoped for renewal—a kind of lesser happiness—in moving upstate. A fantasy that seemed unlikely to withstand the bleak limitations of his actual life. The ping-pong table was a hulking mass in the dim light from the stairwell. DJ reached for the standing lamp at the end of the couch, had to tip it toward him to reach the switch. The bulb flickered as the lamp righted, and then blew. *Tuh.* The confusion of the past was inescapable. In the dream, both Belinda and Sarah were there.

Years after the aneurysm exploded his life, after he'd married Belinda, their days settled into a comfortable if platonic existence, he began having temporal blackouts, periods of lost time. He'd be at work at the downtown Borders one minute, then find himself, hours later, playing pinball at an arcade in Times Square. The death he'd escaped come back home to roost—or so they'd all feared. A threat that led him to start smoking again; led Belinda to a helpless anger, over his smoking, and a depressive despair;

led Sarah to confess that, despite their yearslong friendship, her romantic feelings had never gone away.

She'd been the one to take him to Columbia Presbyterian to see a hotshot neurologist. A referral she wheedled from the shrink helping her stabilize from her own explosion—a manic episode triggered by antidepressants. They were a pair, he and Sarah, with their misfiring brains, and it didn't seem wise to her—or Belinda—that he go anywhere alone. If he sank down into himself, he could still feel Belinda's hand on his cheek before she left for work that morning. Could feel Sarah's hand on his chest, a reluctant dissuasion, before he kissed her a few hours later. Neither one, to him, exclusive of the other somehow.

Their affair lasted only a few weeks before Belinda found out and, despite his promise otherwise, carried on for a few months after, if with less intensity. What time he had with Sarah, they spent in bed at her Upper East Side apartment, eating rice pudding and hot turkey sandwiches delivered from a nearby diner. A perfect existence of sex and food she insisted was not real life.

DJ wanted Sarah's promise that she'd marry him before he left Belinda, while imagining—assuming, really—she'd still be part of his life. He could hardly abandon Belinda, after all she'd done. Sarah had her own conditions. That he leave Belinda first, then "they'd see." That he make enough money to support himself because she couldn't— she wouldn't—take care of him that way. He'd leaned on Belinda, it was true. But with Sarah, with his life gifted back to him by a PET scan and a simple prescription for Dilantin, DJ felt he could do anything. In the end, she decided for them both by abruptly moving to California.

Lost in the dream's lingering wake, DJ hadn't shut off his alarm, which rang now, its nonsensical melody bouncing him back to Hurley.

"I'm making scrambled," Connie called down. "You want?"

No, he tried to say, but his throat constricted with his morning cough.

"Deej? Don't go back to sleep, okay?"

Undeterrable was the word that rose into his mind, but of course she had to press on.

"I'm up," he called. "No eggs though." He rubbed his face and sat up, grabbed yesterday's jeans from the floor and slid them on, a cache of bitter anger tightening his chest. Not for Sarah's leaving back then, which he came to see as a necessary part of her own recovery. It was her recent return, her final destruction of a sustaining possibility that he couldn't forgive.

The first few years after their affair, DJ sent Sarah handwritten letters along with CD mixes of songs he knew she'd like. He rented a PO box so she could send him things, too, and continued to see her when the home textiles market brought her back to New York each spring and fall. They'd meet in Manhattan for coffee or lunch, take long walks through the ever-changing city, but she wouldn't sleep with him—even the few times there'd been a place they could go. Eventually, she refused to see him at all, saying she didn't want to be that person—whether Belinda knew or not. He missed her, but it wasn't the worst thing, more a chapter's end.

For all the hopes he'd once pinned on Sarah, Belinda would prove, again and again, to be his truer match. They became as close, as physically intimate, as was possible outside a sexual sphere—the strain of his affair, the stress of life, her own struggle with antidepressants and their side effects, making an uncrossable divide they'd found a way to live with. The smaller thing in the face of the rest. For Belinda, DJ had always been the one, and she continued to love him, to accept who he was, despite the ways he failed her. But when she died, when he was left alone, his thoughts had returned to Sarah, the love he'd had for her, like an unopened parcel, unchanged.

The sad tenor of his initial call gave way to renewed connection and a growing excitement in the ones to follow.

She'd been thinking of moving back east—everyone had a dream of what, with a little work, his apartment could be—and they talked about her moving in. Then she arrived in Brooklyn, for a preliminary weekend, and their plans fell apart.

Where he grieved Belinda, Sarah grieved who they might've been. Before his marriage, before his aneurysm, all the way back to the sweetness and promise they'd felt at nineteen. Even the life in New York they all might've continued if she and DJ hadn't had an affair. It was what Belinda's death had brought home to her. They had sex— the saddest sex of his life—and for all her tears, all the love Sarah claimed she still felt, she refused to see the man he'd become as anything more than a friend—a hurt that would not go away.

"It's the same as before," she said. "I wouldn't get you. There'd always be Belinda." Lying naked beside him, she noted the mounds of clothing, the oxygen tanks that he'd never returned. "As a friend, I'm willing to help you. But if we were together, I couldn't accept it, I couldn't take it on."

His place was a wreck, but how could that be what came between them? For a while they tried it, this being friends, though he didn't buy her explanation. He was sure she loved him, that there'd always be a spark. Even the weekend she came to "dig out" his living room, he was really just waiting for her to come around.

The first thing Sarah wanted to do was throw out the chifforobe.

"Look how much space it takes up," she said, her arms spread wide. "How far it juts into the room. We can get something at Ikea that'll do you much better. If we organize, I think you'll be surprised."

From the hardware store on Fourth Avenue, she picked out cleaning supplies, new dishtowels and potholders, along with a hammer and crowbar. Sitting in the rickety rolling chair at the Formica table that had become Belinda's desk, the audio of her sluggish IBM routed through a series of jacks and adapters to his old stereo speakers, DJ assembled and played a Sarah-specific song list from across the decades, while she began emptying the drawers. Her idea was to carry those out and then break apart the rest, so they'd be able to fit the pieces through the otherwise impassable hallway. But when she asked him to take the first empty drawer down to the curb, he panicked.

"I can't," he said.

"Sure you can."

"I don't want to," he said, and began to cry. She got mad, banged around in the kitchen for a while, then came back with two cups of coffee. "Here's what we'll do. We'll throw out what's definitively garbage, yeah? Dried up markers and glue and pens. Old bills and magazines. Then we'll condense what's worth keeping and cram as much other stuff into this thing as we can." She patted the side of the cluttered piece with placating reassurance. "But in a way that you can still see what there is and use it."

Then a couple of things happened.

First, Sarah slid a damp paper towel under the chifforobe, to clear away the thicket of dust, and came out with a dead mouse so desiccated it was like a little mouse-shaped piece of suede. She screamed and threw it down, which was alarming and then kind of funny.

"So helpful," she said. "You're a real prince."

He laughed, but didn't get up, and she carried on.

And then, as she was sorting through the papers on the upper shelves, she came across two things that stopped her. A check he'd never cashed from the boutique law firm where Belinda worked as a legal secretary, and the original illustration Sarah had done for a magazine. A small gouache painting, on thick watercolor paper, of a jukebox encircled by 45s.

One corner of the painting was creased to the point of tearing, and something dirty, like the bottom of a carton, had been scraped across the rest. Sarah stepped down from the chair she'd been standing on, a '50s style dining chair whose red vinyl seat she'd made pristine with Formula 409. Standing in the middle of his living room, items she'd pulled from the shelves and drawers scattered at her feet, she seemed only now to notice how filthy her hands had become, and carefully set the illustration down on a clean sheet of paper towel.

"I gave that to you," she said.

"I know."

"You don't care about any of this, do you."

It wasn't a question. "I only care about you."

She sat on the chair, used her forearm to wipe her brow. "That's not going to happen."

"Then why did you come?"

They continued to argue, and it felt as if he'd never known her at all. He turned back to his music and she returned to the kitchen, determined to clean something up.

Declaring a truce, they took the subway into the city, where DJ insisted on springing for dinner at Morimoto. He still had the greater part of the money from Belinda's insurance back then—money that was his to spend, to enjoy how he wanted.

"It's too much," Sarah said.

"It's one meal."

"While Rome is burning, is that it?"

In a tempting singsong, he said, "*The food here is really good…*"

She closed her menu. "And there it is."

"You're against eating now?"

Elbows on the table, as if in exhaustion, Sarah rested her head in one hand. "How many times did you come here with Belinda?"

Her boss had taken them once, in honor of Belinda's birthday, and she'd brought him back, several months later, to celebrate his.

"Twice," he said. "So what?"

"I'm not her. I can't fill her place."

"No one's asking you to."

"No?"

"She's part of my life."

"And she used to be part of mine—you seem to forget that. It was a stupid idea."

"What was?" He reached for her arm, but she sat up, leaned away from the table.

"Dinner. Us. Your fucking chifforobe. Being friends— should I go on?"

DJ tried and tried to explain—the way he saw them, the way she'd held a place in his heart, long before he met Belinda. But it was a place they couldn't find their way back to. "I'm sorry about your painting."

"I know."

"And the mouse."

"*Sooo* disgusting." She brought a fist to her mouth, failed to stifle a giggle. "Oh, my God—your place—" she said, laughing harder. "It's such—can I just say it? It's such a *mess.*"

"Got that out of your system?"

"Whew—sorry." She wiped her eyes, then started laughing again.

Knowing he was losing her, DJ wondered if there'd been a time that he loved her more.

They stayed, ordered cocktails, then a three-course meal, and though it was clearly more than she wanted to spend, he didn't fight her on splitting the check. They'd spoken by phone a few more times, but, entrenched on their opposite coasts, he never saw her again. The chifforobe, on the other hand, had been carefully wrapped in moving blankets and loaded into the truck along with everything else—as if he was ever going to live anywhere else it would fit. He should've let Sarah break it apart, lain the pieces by the curb from whence it came. What had keeping it bought him?

5

"Hell *and* the hand basket," Connie said, when DJ finally made it upstairs, sunlight cascading through the window above the kitchen sink as he poured himself a cup of coffee.

"How's that?"

"Morning," said Elise. She'd been reading a library book, a last bite of toast on the plate beside her. She patted her head, and DJ reached up to his and smoothed down his hair.

"Get your things together, sweetie. I need to talk to your uncle for a sec."

"Whatever," said Elise.

"Most annoying word in the English language," said Connie. "Right up there with *fine*."

DJ stepped aside as she poured the rest of the coffee into a car cup, banged the filter and grounds into the garbage below the sink.

"A slight change of plan."

"You heard from David."

Connie grimaced and shook her head. "Former patient." She clasped a hand to her mouth, shook her head again. Never one to hold her tongue, this gave DJ a terrible feeling. "He got ahold of some pills. Seventeen years old."

"I'm so sorry."

"Yeah. I'll drop Elise, but then I'm going straight in—you'll have to meet me later at the bank."

"So, I'll take David's car. What's he gonna to do?"

"Little problem with that." She raised her chin and DJ followed her gaze toward the door that led to the carport.

"*No,*" he said, then stepped outside. It had rained at some point in the night, and the pavement glittered like a deliberate taunt. As he walked down the slick blacktop, the dry silhouette left from David's Camry came into view, and he couldn't help looking up and down the street, though he knew it was futile.

Connie waited for him in the kitchen doorway. "Anything else you want to tell me?"

"He joked about selling it, but I didn't think … "

Connie's eyes closed, her lips taut, but she didn't speak.

"How is this my fault?"

"It's not," she said, ushering him back inside. "I'm the one who married him."

They're a whole crew, Connie explained, people David had grown up with, who now spanned a spectrum from legitimate to shady, Skip the most darkly enterprising. Not a dealer himself, but he'd been David's coke connection, a man she wouldn't put anything past.

"When things fall apart," she said, "people tend to go backwards. And these guys? They've got a boyhood loyalty, an old ledger of favors I could never decode. Forget about standing between them."

Connie had been the girl most likely to climb out a window, the wildest of her own bunch, doing her share of adolescent drinking and drugs. DJ didn't know how she'd turned into this stanchion of responsibility, this weary, but unfailing dispenser of care to any number of people. She left David yet another message, saying when she'd be at the bank, if he deigned to join her, and that DJ would pick up Elise.

Housed in one of the old canopied storefronts in the Stockade District, unnervingly close to the antiques store,

47

Connie's branch had retained the building's historic exterior. But through the glass he could see the back of her head and shoulders where they rose above the square frame of a generically modern upholstered chair. Facing her, behind an equally characterless desk, sat a woman in a navy suit jacket and one of those silk blouses that tie in a bow at the neck. Relieved he didn't have to face David, DJ's disappointment was massive, nonetheless. Like him, David was—or at least he had been—a giver of great gifts, a man of grand gestures, and DJ knew him to be especially fond of the last-minute save. He scanned the street for the truck. Better than watching the branch manager—or whoever she was—lean forward at her desk, a manila folder turned so that Connie could follow as the woman ran her finger along the text of a document she appeared to be reading aloud. Each time she paused to glance up at his sister, it made DJ bristle. Connie had said only to meet her here, and though he'd be warmer waiting inside, he couldn't bring himself to go in. He lit up and stamped his feet. Whatever the news was, it didn't look good.

All Connie said, when she came out of the bank, was, "Will you drive?"

"Sure. Where'd you—okay."

She was already steps ahead of him. DJ wanted to stop her, make her put on her coat, but he simply caught up, giving way for her sudden turn at the corner, hustling along beside her for the next two blocks. Grateful for a red light, he bent forward to catch his breath.

At the car, she unlocked the passenger side door and held out the keys. He started to ask if they should get something to eat, but she bowed her head and closed her eyes as though she were breathing through a physical pain.

"I'll just take you back, then—all right?"

DJ got in, adjusted the mirrors and inserted the key, but hesitated to start the car. Connie opened the glove box, then clicked it shut without taking anything out. "I knew."

"What? What did you know?"

"Not specifically," she said, mincing the word. "But that niggling feeling. You tell yourself, *Nah*—everything looks good. Even though you know—you know it's all going," she held her thumb and forefinger a tiny bit apart, "just a little too easily according to plan. But I never..."

DJ waited for her to go on.

"Even now," she said, "I'm sure he thinks he can just fix this, right? That's what contractors do."

"Can he?"

Connie looked at him, her expression startled, as though the idea were just making itself fully clear, then quietly said, "No. The house is already in foreclosure."

"How can that be?"

"Not one, not two, but four months behind. Forty-eight hundred bucks—that's a hefty ticket. But the amount doesn't matter. Not as far as the bank's concerned. It's the number of *payments* you miss that counts. And after three, they're well within their rights to take your house. It's all there in the not-so-fine print."

"What about your rights?"

"Forfeited by nonpayment within the terms of the mortgage."

"But—"

"There's no but, DJ. No what about ifs, no couldn't I just—no isn't it possible, either. I just danced all those numbers myself." As if tracing a small tornado, she'd wound a finger through the air, and DJ thought of himself, standing outside the bank, watching the scene as though it were something on TV.

"What there *is*," she went on, "is no compensation for what we put in, all the fucking effort of the past twelve years. In this market, we'd be lucky to get half what the house was worth—but to walk away with nothing? As if walking away isn't hard enough. Can you please just take me back to work? I can't talk, I can't think about this now."

After he dropped Connie off, DJ looped back to the house she'd shared with David. Neither the Camry nor the truck was parked outside, and he didn't know what he'd meant to do if they had been. Still, he idled out front for a while, foolishly imagining all the things he would and wouldn't have said to David.

Connie had told him she'd borrowed money from both Gretchen and Denise to make the down payment on the house where she and Elise were living now, that she'd expected to get that back and more when this one sold, but he didn't know what losing it meant in the larger picture. What he felt, above all else, was stupid. Stupid in trusting David to come through, stupid for not knowing what to say to Connie, stupid for coming back to Hurley. Of course she'd taken him in when he asked. How could she have said no? He'd never considered—not that she'd have admitted it—that her own circumstances might not be stable.

He would need to step up, she'd expect him to, but the thought of getting some crappy job was hard to bear. The monotony was enough to kill you, and all the petty bullshit that went along with kowtowing to bosses—or being one. Even with the storage space hanging over his head, he'd still thought he could coast for a while. How many offers to roll over his credit had he tossed aside, its own little shale-like tower among the piles? But he hadn't wanted that reserve—no safety net, no escape hatch, no out. He'd wanted to press hard into something that would break him to pieces. Only, when it came down to it, he'd merely dangled one foot over the edge, then let the women in his life, in this case Tracy and Connie, cushion his fall.

DJ tried to think of the times that he had stepped up. The jobs he'd gotten and held for as long as he could, across the years of his marriage, reluctantly—even inadvertently—climbing the corporate ladder of bookstore chains, from part-time clerk to full-time manager. There was the small used bookstore in Park Slope—he'd taken that place over and set it on its feet, until the owner had caved to real estate pressure. A disappointment that still surfaced in dreams where he'd find himself yelling at that soft-spoken man, *Why couldn't you hold on?*

And there was Belinda, of course, in those final years. He may have let their apartment go to hell, but he'd been with her every day. Taken her in taxis to treatment and consultations, administered morphine and all the other useless drugs, doing any and everything he could to ease her suffering, her fear. All the way down to the final hour. What did David, what did Connie know of that?

Forty-eight hundred dollars was chump change. One hundred thousand dollars—now *that* was a giddy sum. One that had granted his boon of freedom. DJ had done what he wanted, lived how he wanted, bought what he wanted for a couple of years. He was still angry, would always be angry at what he'd lost—that Belinda had gotten sick, that he'd been left without her.

As for his brief epoch of financial liberty, that beautiful spending down of the money from her insurance was a petulant spit in the eye of the universe, an absolute pronouncement of who he was, who he'd always been, in the clearest and most dire of moralistic-fable terms. He would fiddle and dance all summer long, winter come what may. What did it matter? Who did he matter to? The truth was he hadn't thought any of those things. He'd lived—that was what he'd done. He'd gone on living. Not that he wished

51

he'd died instead, only that all things being equal, nothing seemed equal at all. Which made no sense. It was just … it was just here he was.

The mall hadn't been part of DJ's landscape growing up, and living in Brooklyn, he'd bought all his clothes in thrift stores or what seemed the last Army Navy store left in New York. But browsing the racks in H&M with Elise, seeing the things that drew her eye, he understood that shopping, of all things, was what he missed: the casual company of wandering through a store with someone he cared for, as though his whole life hung on the balance of the words, *What do you think about this?* Elise set her backpack down by a rack of hats and tried on a straw one with an enormous brim.

"Ta-da," she said, striking a hieroglyphic pose. One hand jauntily placed on her hip, the other held palm up, wrist and elbow bent, one flexed foot lifted off the ground. DJ smiled, recalled the figurine that Belinda loved, still safely bubble-wrapped and further cushioned by the clothes in his duffel. Probably a better gift than the marbled egg, were it something he could part with.

"You should get it," he said.

"*Nooo.* Too silly."

"Well, you should get something."

Elise picked up a gray wool porkpie hat with a black band. She put it on, looked in the mirror, and then tipped it slightly back on her head.

"Oh, now *that*," said DJ, "is you."

She looked effortlessly stylish in an offbeat way, making him feel he'd just seen a flash of the person she'd grow up to be. Elise rolled her eyes, but he could tell she liked the hat. She took it off, started to look at the tag.

"Don't do that—give it here."

"I don't really need it."

"But you want it."

"You already got me a gift."

"That was different."

"How?"

"I don't know. This is Friday—Friday buy-your-niece-a-hat day." DJ flipped the tag over. "It's only nineteen bucks."

"Nineteen ninety-nine."

"Plus tax—I thought you wanted to come here."

"Just to look."

"Just looking's no fun."

"It's like my *dad*," said Elise, her voice raised, then immediately dropping, so he barely caught the words. "I know you don't have money."

DJ brushed his hand along the soft wool of the hat. "Your mom told you that?"

"She said … she said you were moving up here because you couldn't afford to live in Brooklyn anymore, but my dad said you blew through all your money—same thing she says that *he* does. Not to me—but I've heard her say it. On the phone."

"No one can afford to live in Brooklyn anymore." DJ shook his head. He didn't want to think about David—or whoever Connie had been talking to. "Listen, E. I did get myself in a … situation. And your mom, she is—she's bailing me out. If you wanted a *car,* I couldn't do it." DJ paused, sick at his example—*a car? A house? What else couldn't he buy her?*—then he stumbled on. "A twenty-dollar hat isn't gonna break me, okay? You could go your whole life and not find a hat that really suits you. I'm gonna walk over to that register right now so we can impress the cashier with your savvy taste."

"E," she said. "I like that."

"Nice choice," said the cashier, and DJ looked at Elise, as if to say *see?*

The look she returned was a playful sneer. "What happened to my dad's car, anyway?"

Connie must've said something about why he was picking her up, but he'd no idea what.

"What'd your mom say?"

"I'm asking you."

"So you are."

The cashier gave DJ his card back with a curious glance he did his best to ignore.

"I guess he took it. I'm not really sure."

"Did they have a fight?"

"No ... not exactly."

The cashier held the hat out between them. "Would you like a bag, or will you wear it out?"

"Wear it—thanks." Elise hefted her backpack onto her shoulders, set the hat on her head, and made the same adjustment, as if she'd owned it for years. She led the way as they wove through the racks of clothing and stepped into the concourse. She hesitated, as though uncertain which way to go, then turned back to DJ. "Did *you*?"

He could've pretended he didn't know what she meant, but there seemed no point.

"Depends on who you ask."

"Thank you," Elise said. "And for the hat."

The afternoon had trickled by, much of it spent in the food court, Elise doing homework, DJ surfing the web and wishing he could smoke, the half-finished melody he'd been toying with looping through his brain, the mall a wash of other echoing sound and conversation. When they picked Connie up, she'd given him a warning glance, then carried on like any ordinary evening when they stopped for burgers at a redone restaurant that was once the Italian place their parents had favored. As she said his first day back, things had changed and they hadn't.

They drove home to find David's truck parked by the bottom of the driveway, the star light in the carport an unsettling beacon. Connie pulled up but made no move to get out.

"You want me to take Elise for a spin around the block?"

"So you don't have to be here?"

"Well, that too."

"What's going on?" said Elise. "What'd he do?"

Connie turned to face her. "You dad didn't keep up the payments on our old house."

Her frankness left DJ stunned. At breakfast she'd made Elise leave the room, and now—well, now, he supposed, she could hardly keep it a secret.

"What does that mean?"

"Well," said Connie. "I haven't quite figured that out. Let's just go inside, all right? Okay, oops—there he is."

Elise got out, DJ and Connie slower to follow.

"You guys gonna sit in the driveway all night? Nice hat, Lisey—what up?" David said, giving way as she brushed past. "No hug for your dad?"

"Let her be," said Connie.

"What'd you say to her?"

"Can we not do this in the driveway?"

"One day," he said to DJ. "You couldn't keep your mouth shut?"

"*David,*" said Connie.

"All right," he said, all nonchalance, his arm extended like a maître d. "*Entrez, entrez.* Let's go in your house. You too, *mon ami.*"

It was obnoxious, to say the least, but all DJ could think was, *He doesn't know about the house.* He tried to catch Connie's eye, but she made a beeline for the sink, saying she needed a glass of water. David leaned on the kitchen rail and DJ hovered near the door as though suspended, until she turned around.

"You sold your car?"

"Not sold. But traded. Yeah."

"*Jesus, David.*"

"*Jesus, yourself,*" he said. "To a carpenter—for man-hours—so I'll have more cash in hand from the job I bid on yesterday, which I landed, thank you very much. I wouldn't have gotten shit for that thing otherwise. I just came by for the keys and to give you that." He nodded toward the table, where a thick white envelope rested against the saltshaker. "I was about to give up and leave a note. Twenty-four hundred bucks. Ought to keep the wolves at bay—since you couldn't wait."

Connie looked at DJ in disbelief. He started to move toward her, but she held up her hand, turned her attention to David.

"The house..." she cleared her throat twice, then let out a short bark of a laugh. "Look at that—I can't even say it."

"Say what?"

"The *house* is in foreclosure."

"That can't be right."

"And yet it is. At least you won't have to finish repairing the fucking porch now."

"You have to know how to talk to these guys, Connie. I screwed up. I was late—I'm sorry, all right? I'll go down there tomorrow and straighten it out."

"*You can't fix this,*" she said, her voice ringing through the house.

DJ heard a door open in the hall.

"*Mom?*"

"It's okay, Lisey—I'm all right."

In bare feet and a long tie-dyed sleep shirt, Elise padded into the kitchen, nestled up beside Connie at the sink. Connie put an arm around her shoulder, and a mix of sorrow and helplessness took away DJ's breath.

"It's a done deal," she said to David in a calm, quiet voice. "I read the contract. You were four months behind."

David pulled out a chair from the kitchen table and sat down.

"Well, fuck me," he said.

Connie winced.

"Sorry."

"You should go. We'll talk tomorrow."

"Connie."

"*Please.*"

David reached for the envelope and stood up. "You got my car keys?"

"*DJ*," Connie said.

"Right—sorry," he said, heading to the basement to retrieve them. When he came back up, only David was left, standing by the side door.

"Well, at least she has you now," he said. "For whatever that's worth."

DJ was both stung and alarmed. "Are you going somewhere?"

"Maybe. I don't know." David put his hand out and DJ gave him the keys. "What a mess. This is not what I intended, you know? Things just … well. It doesn't matter, does it?"

Before he could think what to say, David turned and walked out, leaving the door open behind him. DJ stood there, the cold night air spilling in. He tapped his coat pocket where his cigarettes were, but instead of stepping out, he shut the door, took off his coat, and hung it over the rail. He walked down to Elise's room, where she and Connie were talking. But Connie glanced up from the end of the bed, and he understood that he shouldn't go in.

DJ dug through the kitchen drawers until he found a pair of scissors, then brought his duffel to the basement couch. He freed the bubble-wrapped figurine from its cocoon of

T-shirts, cut the tape and carefully unwound the plastic trappings. When he came to the bottom-most layer, he heard a little clink. One of the dancer's arms had broken off at the elbow where it had been glued before. For a long time, she'd graced the Formica table in their living room, but tended to get knocked over, and eventually Belinda set her atop the shallow bookshelf by her side of the bed. *Keeping good company*, she said, with a poodle-base lamp she'd bought for a dollar at a stoop sale and a zebra thumb-puppet DJ had given her when they were first going out. Treasured objects overshadowed in time by an ever-growing battalion of medications, Advil and Rescue Remedy giving way to what she liked to call *the harder stuff*. Looking around the basement for a safe spot to stand the dancing figure now, DJ heard the soft question mark of Connie calling his name from the top of the stairs.

"Present," he called back.

"Can I come down?"

He tipped his head back to see her through the rise of balusters. *"Mi casa, su casa,"* he said, with immediate regret. "Too soon?"

"Sooner, later," she said, coming down the stairs. "All the same."

He stuffed the shirts strewn across the couch back into the duffel, motioned for her to sit down.

"What happened here?"

The figurine lay on the loose bubble-wrap on the coffee table, and DJ opened his own hand to reveal the small, flexed ceramic one. "Failed protection."

"Can I see?" She picked up the dancer. "I don't remember her. But then, your place…"

"Really? You're going to go there?"

"No," she said, an aggrieved exhale. "Not tonight. Belinda's?"

"I bought it for her, but yeah."

She ran her finger over the rough edge. "What'd you use before?"

DJ shrugged. Belinda had fixed it.

"Ah. Elise has Gorilla. That should do the trick. It all starts out so well, doesn't it?" She gathered the bubble-wrap into a neater pile, then set the dancer back down.

"So," he said, "what happens now?"

Connie slumped back into the couch. "I'm taking Monday morning off so I can see the lawyer and he can give me shit for not staying in the house."

"How come you didn't?"

"*How come?*" She lifted her head, turning toward him in irritated disbelief. "Because I had a bigger vision. Because it made the most sense. It still does. Except for David fucking it up. *That house.*"

"*Aaaah!*" he said, a mock wail of fear. "*Sorry, sorry, sorry.*"

"No, no—it's what people expect. The classic bitter joke, how the wife gets the house. But I wasn't getting the house—neither of us were getting the house. And I didn't want Elise skulking around those old corners and cubbyholes, hoping we'd come back together as a family someday."

The words gave DJ a funny feeling, as though he'd left Belinda to wander through their emptied rooms, the building due to be demolished for all he knew. Wasn't that what he'd been doing? No matter where he was, or who he was with? Irrationally waiting, with each day that drew by, for the return of his wife? Or was it simply that he, who could go anywhere, wanted only to go back to Belinda? Death leaving her nowhere and everywhere at once.

"I got a ridiculous deal on this place," Connie went on. "I felt like a vulture, I promise you, scooping up the remains. My own freedom, whatever scrap of security, resting on some other couple's financial misery. Even my guilt feels like hubris now."

"It's hubris just to be *alive*."

"What the fuck am I going to tell Gretchen and Denise?" She shook her head. "I just wanted to move forward. You can't rent a two-bedroom apartment that's not a hole for less than twelve hundred bucks, and the mortgage here is less than half that. Against the advice of legal counsel," she said acidly, "I bought this place and covered Elise's expenses. David paid the higher mortgage and was working on the house. We were spending the least possible amount of money until it sold and then we'd have a clean break, each of us walking away with something. This place for me, and for David a chunk of cash to put into the business or something of his own. We were so close to free and clear. I can't understand it. Or maybe I understand all too well. My believing he could hold up his end? Assuming everything was okay? Now that's a failure of protection."

"We all have our blind spots."

"Wisdom from the wise," she said, and then, "Sorry. I didn't mean that."

"It's all right. I'm used to it by now."

Her shoulders hunched forward as she started to cry.

"*Connie—noo.* C'mon—it's okay, we're okay."

"*I'm just…*" she pressed her palm against her forehead, then wiped it across each side of her face. "I'm just so *mad.*"

"I know," he said. "I know."

As they sat together, on the couch from their parents' den, a peaceful silence bloomed. Only a cigarette could've made it a more perfect moment of respite. Connie had closed her eyes and, he thought, drifted off, her exhaustion palpable but her presence deeply comforting. For most of his adult life, Gretchen and Denise had been more like distant relatives than sisters. But Connie, he understood now, he had missed, and while he'd dropped any number of other people with little if any regret, he wished he hadn't cut her from his life these last few years. Thinking how much it must've hurt her, he felt his own tears rise and was startled when she spoke.

"I really did plan on giving you time to find your feet."

Of course she hadn't been sleeping—she'd been busy turning the squares of her predicament like a Rubik's cube.

"Were you serious about selling your records?"

What about the money in that envelope, he thought better of asking. "I could be."

Yesterday, the idea of selling them had felt heroic. But now, when it came down to it—when she was asking him to—a flush of anxiety made him crack his neck. The hollow ceramic fragment was still in his hand. He placed it beside the dancer, in line with its proper angle. How strange that the figurine should break again and again at the elbow joint and not the more worrisome tip of her long-peaked and gold-painted hat.

"DJ?" Connie leaned forward, compelling him to face her. "You're on board with this, right? Because you're gonna have to pick up Elise for the next … " Her hand fluttered up and then fell. "Anyway—*he's* not driving her, and I need my car, so we're gonna have to get you something. Things are hard enough on Elise—I'm not putting her on that Goddamn school bus."

"All right."

"What?"

"Nothing. I just don't get it. We took the bus."

"You overlapped—you never rode alone."

DJ thought about this. "Did something happen to you? What happened?"

Shame came off her, like a radiant heat. "Nothing happened to me."

"*Oh, Constance,*" he said. "What'd you do?"

The sound she let out was a half-moaning half-disgusted sigh. "She was just a girl. A plain, ordinary girl. Little chubby.

Freckled face and arms. Feathery bangs hanging over wire-rim glasses. Shy. She was shy. And we took her apart. Me and my little posse of friends. Bit by bit, ride by ride. Some days leaving her just enough alone that she could think it was over. But it never was, on and on, until the end of the year. We had a *song,* DJ. A fucking song to make fun of her, okay?"

"Okay, okay."

"I see these kids at work and they're just ... they're caught. Horrible situations—any sane person would swallow a bottle of pills. And logically—logically I know that's not the bus. But it feels so *grim*—that long noisy ride— you don't remember this? The stopping and waiting? That insanely circuitous route?"

"The closest kids always dropped off last."

"*Yes.*" Connie slapped the couch.

"What'd you do before?"

"Before all of *this?*" she said, her hand sweeping back up, "we used to carpool with another family—Elise spent half her afternoons at Jenn's anyway. Parents separated a little before we did—that complicated the driving, but it worked. Then about a month ago, their divorce goes through, Jenn's mom gets full custody, and moves to Connecticut—smack in the middle of the school year. It looked like the bus for Elise, but David steps right up, brings her to the job site if need be. I thought it was good— them spending more time. Brilliant idea *that* was—what a great mom am I." Connie took a deep breath, then blew the air out through her lips, as though the explanation, as much as the events, had drained her. "Jenn was Elise's one good friend. I keep asking her if she wants to visit, but she seems set on toughing it out."

"*Ouch,*" DJ said.

"It's not going to kill her to take the bus. But why should she? Everything else is changing for her. Why can't this one thing stay the same?"

"It will. She won't. What do you want me to say?"

"Aren't you gonna want a car anyway?"

"Probably," he said, though—living in Brooklyn—the idea of a car was always to get away, and it seemed a pity to buy one now, when he had no money and nowhere to go. "Was that it?"

"It's as far as I've got." Connie sank back into the couch. "You buy a house, you have a kid, and day after day your life spins by. Work, meals, bedtime stories. Fucking milk going bad in the fridge. You remember too little. You remember too much." She patted the cushion between them. "You gonna ever open this up?"

"It could happen," he said.

She laughed, a sharp dazzling surprise, and whatever came next, he felt he'd done something right.

6

DJ's collection of guitars had not started out as such, they'd simply been the guitars he played. An acoustic, an electric, and the sentimental holdover of a 12-string from the '70s. He wouldn't accumulate, he'd merely trade up, selling off what he had to attain something finer. And then, in the early years of his marriage, they'd had people over so often—who played, or sang, or could at least carry a basic harmony—that it seemed only natural to have a second guitar around.

It was really the advent of Craigslist that led him astray. If you had to go into a music store, have the clerk pull an instrument down from a ceiling rack, reveal your meager chops in a roomful of kid-prodigies and studio musicians, it made you less inclined. But to amble over to someone's apartment, maybe jam with them for a little while, hear the story behind their giving up a prized guitar, was a temptation he found hard to resist. It was interesting just to see how other people lived, and when Belinda died, it was a salve for his loneliness.

The woman he'd bought the Martin from was a talented musician and contemporary composer—an academic with a Patti Smith vibe—who'd turned out to be dying herself. For a month or so, they'd joined their sorrows. He'd have paid more for the guitar, would've bought her baby grand and the beautiful Persian rug beneath it, if he'd had somewhere to put them. He'd have moved in, which they'd briefly considered one rainy afternoon, nestled on her couch, listening across the spectrum from Satie to The Pogues to Miles Davis. She was one of those people who could play almost any instrument she picked up. He'd told no one about her, or the time they'd spent, or how hard they'd both wept when she insisted he move on.

As the guitars began to accumulate, Tracy, who'd disapproved of so little else, disdained his haphazard care of them. She'd lent him a couple of quality stands, though he still tended to lean guitars against whatever was available—a chair, a shelf, the end of his bed. Like so much else in his life, a case could be made for his indiscriminate choices, a series of impulses he seemed unable to control, reflecting time, money, and attention he perhaps shouldn't have spent. And yet, each of those instruments had something unique and undeniable.

Like the many guitars that often went unplayed, there were months he didn't see Tracy at all, her time sunk into a recording project or simply a new girlfriend. Her life was always chockablock with work and travel, with lovers and other friends, but she had a way of showing up in a crisis like nobody else—a debt he'd done little to repay.

In the first dark bubble of his grief, Tracy had slept beside him, kind in her refusal of more than one attempt to extend their intimacy beyond conversation. Saying nothing about his side of the bed—the wastebasket overflowing with takeout containers, empty cookie and potato chip bags; the ashtray with its impressive mound of soft gray powder and butts; an ever-growing collection of near-empty glasses and soda bottles battling for the last inch of his nightstand—she simply cleared a path through the piles of dirty clothes to Belinda's side. She put on clean sheets, tidied the things he'd left untouched on Belinda's nightstand, carving out a space among the tchotchkes and pastel Post-its, the amber vials and plastic bottles of pills, to set her phone, her watch, and whatever novel she'd pulled from the bedside bookshelf before drifting off, as he went on watching late-night reruns of classic TV.

He'd come to treasure the way a little cowlick of her darkening blonde hair flopped over her forehead, the precise, freshly shaven V at the back of her neck, and those graceful hands, genius of console, keyboard, and guitar, tucked under her chin as she slept.

How many times had he thought to call her these past few days? Waiting in the pick-up line for Elise, looping around from Hurley to Kingston in David's Camry, or sitting as he was this morning, in the cave of Connie's basement, his empty stomach grumbling with her strong morning brew, staring at her shelves as if they had something to tell him. His muted phone sat on the coffee table before him, beside the tube of glue Elise had silently delivered, the damaged figurine still lying helpless on her pile of bubble wrap.

Tracy's packing him out had been a line too far, their final goodbye outside his building a tearful parting. A two-hour drive upstate and he felt more distant than when she traveled to India the year before, and couldn't help wondering if she too wanted him to move on. It kept him from calling. If he waited long enough, she'd call—the guilty apology his area of expertise. A crappy way of going about things, in which he could almost take pride. *This is me. I'm that guy. Take it or leave it.* An out that had served him well enough; a habit he wasn't sure he could—or that he wanted to—break. What was the point of trying, of changing now? It wasn't like he hadn't disappointed everyone he knew— the best defense was to keep people's expectations low. He should make a T-shirt.

Careful not to bump the table, DJ pulled his guitar case up and over the arm of the couch. Each stiff clasp opened with a satisfying snap, the Gibson's body a familiar comfort against his own as he turned the pegs. *Five minutes,* Connie called down. He set the half-tuned guitar back into the velvet-lined case. It was much too early to call Tracy, anyway.

He always started out with high hopes, determined to keep his word, to hold up his end. But over time, each promise grew heavier than the last, as though the promises themselves were the problem, and not his quitting, or his spending, or the breach of faithfulness they defended against. It was expectation that forever held him down, sent him into a paroxysm of self-destructive resistance. He didn't know how Connie—or even Belinda, in her day—plowed continually forward. Wherever his thoughts rambled, wherever he wished he could be, he was still in Hurley, bound to spend Saturday morning with his sister and niece at Kingston's bi-weekly Farmers Market—as good an evasion as any, for each of them. A little pending doom, Sir, with your Yukon Gold potatoes?

Presuming a meager collection of tents, a handful of people picking through limited offerings, DJ was stunned by the vibrant throng. Wall Street was packed with bannered tables displaying a wide array of local produce, meat and cheese, bread and pastry, honey, chocolate, and preserves, to rival any market in Brooklyn, or even the one in Union Square. Cirrus clouds swept across a pale blue sky, the morning brisk, but not unbearable, an unexpected smell of charcoal grilling in the air. A bluegrass band was tuning up, and DJ again thought of Tracy and his stored guitars, of the banjo Belinda had barely begun to play.

Elise was wearing the pork pie hat but was keeping her distance. He'd thought her only sleepy when she brought down the glue, but now it seemed distinct, as though a mark had been made against him in her books. Regardless of any trouble with, or the absence of, her dad, DJ hadn't considered what it might be like for her, to have him taking up space in their small house, or occupying any part of her mom's already strained time and attention. Connie's hand rested on Elise's shoulder as they navigated the crowd. Startled to feel a hand on his own, DJ whirled around.

"*Hey,*" he said, his pleasure at seeing Andrea overwhelming any notion he might otherwise have had of playing it cool.

"Sorry—I couldn't remember your name."

"DJ."

"Andrea."

"Right."

"Are they with you?"

DJ turned, following her gaze to where Connie and Elise had stalled, people wending around. He waved them back and made introductions. "Andrea works at the store where I got you the marbled egg." Without thinking, he said to Connie, "David did some work for her brother."

Andrea smiled. "David's your husband?

"*Ex,*" Connie said. "About to be."

"Oh—sorry," Andrea looked to DJ for help.

"That's all right," Connie said. "We're all a little..." She too turned to him now, her look one of wry annoyance. "Discombobulated."

"*Wow,*" said Elise. "That's a five-star word. Can I go on ahead?"

"I'll come with you," said Connie. "Deej, you'll catch up?"

"No, no," Andrea said. "I'm already late. You should all come by the store. I'm like a prisoner there. It was nice to meet you. Good to see you again."

"You too," said DJ. Then she slipped into the crowd.

"Unbelievable," said Connie.

"Sorry," he said. "We ran into her, when we—when I..."

68

"On your little jaunt? That's interesting. But it's not what I meant. Less than a week, you've been here, and already…" Her hand drifted out in the direction Andrea had disappeared. "Whatever that was."

DJ hoped it was something but didn't feel like he'd racked up any points. What he did feel, troubling his tentative excitement, was the usual pull on his loyalty—whatever he wanted always at the sake of someone else.

"Can we *please* get some breakfast now?" said Elise. "Before they sell out of scones?"

"Are you coming with us?" said Connie. "Or will you be buying more paperweights?"

"That's hardly fair."

The smile she gave him tore at his heart. "Nothing ever is."

While it was tempting, oh, so tempting, DJ didn't go, or drag Connie and Elise with him, to the antiques store. It was enough, for now, to enjoy the thrum of anticipation, the thinnest thread of possibility, without plunging ahead. By letting it sit, he could turn his focus and fealty to those he'd come in with, his enjoyment buoyed by Andrea's invitation. After their fill of breakfast pastries and additional caffeine, even Connie seemed to lighten up, the festive atmosphere hard to resist. The band was surprisingly good—not solely bluegrass but tinged with alternative. He'd forgotten the musical enclave that Kingston could be. One of the guitar players was exceptional, his voice rough, but emotionally resonant, and DJ found himself moved.

"Can you play like that?" Elise asked.

"Like that?" he said. "No."

"Oh, I don't know," said Connie. "Your uncle wasn't bad in his day."

Elise nodded, and as he had the first time they'd gone into Kingston, and then earlier today, DJ had a sense of her as a keen observer, someone keeping track.

Connie hoisted the canvas bag of produce higher on her shoulder.

"You want me to carry that?" he said.

"Nah. I'm all right." She checked her phone, and he knew, by the twitch of a frown, she was waiting to hear from David. She ran a hand through her hair, then widened her eyes and smiled. "Did you want to swing by your storage unit on the way home?"

"What?" he said.

"It's just up this way, right? On 28?"

She knew he was renting storage. Part of his promise not to be too much of a burden on her life—not that he'd literally said that, but the underlying gist. He just didn't remember when or why he would've told her *where*. Those last days in his apartment...had Tracy spoken to her?

"Unless you already have a clear idea of what you've got," Connie was saying now. "I could drop you off for a while, come and get you later. I thought I'd make some calls, see if anyone I know has a lead on a car, before we turn to a lot or the classifieds."

"Is this your records?" said Elise. "What you were asking that guy?"

"I don't have a pen or anything."

"A pen?" Connie snorted. "You need a pen?"

"Pen, paper. A box cutter."

"What guy?" she said to Elise.

"The nosy clerk at Rhino Records. Can I go with you?"

"You don't want some time to yourself?" Connie said.

"I'm all right."

"Deej?"

"I don't even have the key."

Connie snickered. "Well, I'm sure they've got an office

70

there. You'll show them your ID and they'll give you the key—isn't that what your friend arranged?"

"I guess. I don't know."

Connie's head fell back as she laughed. "*Oh, my God.*"

"Mom?"

She was still laughing, as though she'd just heard he still believed in the tooth fairy, a mirthful titter, as contagious as it was embarrassing. A relief, despite the tightening of his throat.

"We'd better go by there and figure it out, don't you think? I've probably got a legal pad in the car, and there's a hardware store in Kingston Plaza."

"Do I have a choice?"

She leveled her gaze at him. "You had other plans?"

"Nope," he said. "I did not." His life was not his own.

"Okay, then." Connie patted his back. "Let's get you guys a couple bottles of water."

DJ took a last look at the band, who were setting down their instruments for a break. Now or never, he supposed. Connie was always happiest when things were in motion.

Elise resettled her hat back on her head. "So we're going?"

"Onward, forward," he said.

The crowd had thinned, and Elise strode ahead, one hand sketching figure eights at her side as though she were keeping tempo with a song.

"She's a good kid," Connie said.

DJ nodded, thinking not of Elise but of Connie, maybe five years old, marching around the house quoting Dr. Seuss lines about an elephant saying what he meant, and being faithful one-hundred percent. He should've gone with Andrea when he had the chance.

Most of the people DJ knew in the city rented storage units—no one ever had enough space—and from the

71

elevated subway lines you could see the fading ads on the brick walls of enormous old buildings, housing unimaginable amounts of furniture and who knew what else—the stuff, treasured and not, of hundreds of lives. The television show *Storage Wars*—a competitive auctioning-off of abandoned lockers—had, like several other reality shows, gone inter-national. Though there was little chance of any camera crew showing up at Catskill Park Storage, two flat-topped single-story white buildings with dark green doors, nestled against the barely leafing hills of the Bluestone Wild Forest. It made him think of tennis somehow. Or pool cabanas. Except for the glinting round locks, the gravel drive, and the office, situated in a white clapboard house, across a stretch of still winter-browned lawn.

As Connie predicted, it was easy enough to get the key. He walked around back as she slowly followed with the car, the tires kicking up dust. Hot for March even at midday, the sun beat down on his head as he faced the green expanse of corrugated metal and heard the slam of two car doors, then crunching footsteps, until his little sister and his niece stood on either side of him. He turned the key in the heavy lock, slipped it from its loop.

"Okay," he said. "Here goes nothing." He bent down and gave the door one wrenching heave, sending it upward with the familiar rattle of Brooklyn storefronts facing the new day.

"Whoa," said Elise.

"You're gonna need more than a box cutter," Connie said. "A backhoe, maybe. Jesus Christ."

"Looks like that's what they used to get it in there," said Elise.

DJ could imagine Tracy's close supervision of the packing of the truck, her detailed instructions, the large tip she'd have given the movers, and how hard they would've laughed at the delivery point, eager to reclaim their moving blankets and dump it all off, having met the minimum required of them.

Here and there, crammed in with the ceiling-high wall of boxes and bulging black garbage bags, DJ could glimpse a familiar object. The curving crown of the chifforobe, a stalk-like floor lamp with cone-shaped metal shades, a Fender mini-amp turned on its side. All of it shoved— or possibly tossed—into the unit. Back in Brooklyn, he couldn't bring himself to take out the Goddamn recycling, how was he supposed to deal with this?

"I guess you should've been here," Connie said.

"*Yeah*," he said. "I guess so."

"What do you want to do?"

"Sit down?"

"Must be a chair in there somewhere," said Elise.

DJ laughed, they all did, but then he was crying. "I can't…I don't want…" he looked at Connie. "I'm sorry—"

"No, no, no—c'mon, now. It's all right. We'll help you."

"I'm sorry," said Elise, which only made him cry harder.

"It's okay." DJ swiped at his face with the back of his hand. "It was funny. Please—don't be sorry."

Tracy had wanted him to buy clear bins—like the ones in Connie's basement. And while he'd gone along with most things, he'd been so angry about being forced out, so stubbornly against spending his money on that kind of crappy plastic, so anti-organizational, that he'd flat out refused, relenting only on her purchase of a few to pro-tect Belinda's photographs. It was bad enough to have to buy cardboard boxes, though Tracy had made use of much of his record room pile. Now, of course, he could see her point, for stackability alone, with the jumble before him worse than his own mad creation. It made him think of the stock images he'd seen of crushed car cubes. Thank God she'd held onto his guitars.

"At least everything's labeled," Connie said. She

smoothed out a rumple in a wedged garbage bag, bringing its neatly written label into full view. BLANKETS + B'S FLORAL COMFORTER. "Wow—that's someone who really cares about you."

"She's gay," he said.

"Ah."

"Belinda was always so cold, especially…" he wiped away another welling of tears, determined to get out the words. "She needed an additional layer, and I insisted she splurge on whatever she wanted from The Company Store. I wanted her to be…"

"*Comfortable*," Connie said. "She was."

"There's tissues in the car," said Elise.

"That's all right—I'm all right." He shucked off his jacket, then didn't know what to do with it. "God, it's hot out here, isn't it?"

"It's like the desert," Connie said. "If the desert was next to the woods."

"Or the highway," said Elise.

"So, you didn't sort through anything."

DJ just looked at her.

"Right." Connie stepped up to the building, shielded her eyes from the sun, and rose up on her toes to peer in. "I'd say you could reorganize, but yeah—that's too big a job for just you and Elise. Did she have an army?"

"Something like that."

"Well, you're not going to be looking at any records today. How far back does it go?"

DJ dug into his jacket pocket for the information sheet he'd been given with the key. "Ten by fifteen."

"That's bigger than your room," she said to Elise. "What you need is a second unit."

DJ shook his head.

"But that costs. So lock it up and we'll go home. Have some lunch, make some calls, figure out what you're gonna do."

She checked her phone again, then her eyes met his, and DJ knew they were thinking the same thing: What they could use was David—the way he used to be.

Back at Connie's, DJ folded his clothes and tucked them into the set of plastic drawers beneath the ping-pong table. *At least she has you now,* David had said. DJ closed his eyes, not in prayer so much as a begging wish: *Please do not let him have taken off.* He didn't really imagine David being of any help, though he couldn't banish the picture from his mind; he just didn't think their small circle could handle another hit.

It was one thing to be mad at your dad—it was another for him to disappear. DJ's own father, if a distant and passive figure, had been a constant presence, and though money hadn't been free-flowing—they'd been on the lowest ebb of middle class—their family life, by comparison, had been stable. Quiet. Placid. He'd felt suffocated growing up in his parents' house; a reign of politeness and formality under which most things were left unsaid, the seat, he imagined, of Connie's rebellion. For all her harping and overprotectiveness, he admired and was moved by the close, spirited relationship she had with Elise.

He'd been lucky, the neurosurgeon had said of DJ's aneurysm. To have lived—many people didn't—and not lost more of his memory, though a sizable chunk of his early childhood had, in fact, been wiped out. But the past few days had sent him tumbling at unexpected moments into that hazy past. Gretchen and Denise fighting over who got to push Connie in the stroller, his father standing up from the dinner table, how steep the staircase had once appeared, like something out of Hitchcock's *Vertigo.* A pervasive hush that seemed irreconcilable with a houseful of kids.

There'd been debt, as it turned out, that ate up the

sale of his parents' house—Gretchen the one to handle all of that. Not that he expected any money from them. His father—who'd been a copy editor at the local paper—dead of a heart attack at seventy-six; his mother holding on only for a few years after, still running a crappy vacuum around the downstairs, as though cleaning were the answer to everyone's woes.

Whether his father had once held aspirations of something more, of becoming a reporter or an editor, DJ didn't know. He'd never asked. There'd been a time, as a kid, he believed his father secretly held a more glorious position. That his meek and neutral countenance provided the necessary cover for his being a spy. A memory—better left forgotten—that made him sad for them both.

Connie had made a good choice, moving Elise to this smaller, more affordable home. As far as his living here, that was yet to be seen.

Among the framed photographs dotting the shelves, was an old black-and-white shot of their parents as newlyweds, a trip they'd taken to Niagara Falls that his mother often fondly recalled. "You don't have to go far," she'd say, "but it's nice to get away." And sure enough, here he was, planted in his sister's basement, as though he'd never left Hurley at all. Only now he had a giant locker full of stuff he couldn't afford to maintain, a detail he'd yet to confess to Connie.

Meaning to re-glue the arm of the figurine, he settled on the couch. He picked her up but found his hands too shaky and set her back down on the bed of bubble wrap. Maybe he'd have to sell the Martin after all.

The afternoon was drifting by, DJ still waiting for Connie to call him upstairs. Instead, Elise came softly padding down.

"Are we never having lunch?"

"There's stuff for sandwiches—she said you could make your own."

"How many calls is she making?"

"She's taking a *nap*," Elise said, leaning hard on the word.

"And that's a bad thing because ... ?"

"Because she's not a napping person."

"No—I don't suppose she is. Did you eat?"

"Muenster cheese and tomato."

"A Connie classic."

"She always puts on too much mayonnaise."

"I did not know that."

Elise came around to the other side of the coffee table. "You still didn't glue her?"

"I was going to."

"But then you didn't."

"When you're right, you're right."

Elise picked up the hand of the figurine and he felt a nervous twinge.

"She used to nap a lot," she said, "when we first moved in. But she doesn't now—or she didn't, until today." She glanced around the room, the dancer's hand still in hers. "It's kind of dark in here."

DJ nodded toward the lamp. "One of the bulbs blew out."

"And you didn't replace it."

A small laugh escaped him. "I did not."

"There's bulbs in the laundry room. I'll get you one."

She set the fragment down carefully beside the dancer and walked over to a door he hadn't really registered at the bottom of the stairs. It opened into an even darker space and he felt a draft of cold air. An overhead fluorescent flickered on to reveal a washer and dryer and the tail end of what looked to be a fully loaded set of Metro shelves.

"Just past the Christmas ornaments," Elise called out. "Sixties and hundreds."

"Cobwebby in there," she said, brushing at her head with the back of her wrist as she returned. "And pipes. You'll want to duck."

She put in a new bulb, jingled the broken filament of the old one, then set it on the ping-pong table. DJ followed her gaze back to the figurine.

"That was hers?"

"Yeah. Belinda's. It was."

Elise nodded. "You miss her."

"I do." He thought of David, of Connie napping upstairs, of Elise's friend having moved away. "I could use a pair of steady hands—you feel like helping me glue it?"

"Now that you can see?"

In a parody of being shot, he clasped his hand to his heart. "Last word—is that how it's going to be?"

"Yep."

"I can live with that."

The smile she gave him was lit with irony. "Doesn't seem like you can."

How could you not love this kid? "You may have a point," he said, then scooted over to make room.

The whole thing only took a minute, Elise carefully dabbing each end with glue before he pressed them into place. He was still holding the pieces together when his phone, set to silent, vibrated at the end of the table.

"Ahh!" he said, and Elise snatched it up.

"Tracy. You want me to answer?"

"Send it to voicemail. I'll call her back."

She set the phone down on the arm of the couch beside his cigarettes. "That's your spot for everything, huh?"

She was right. His lighter, his keys, a business card from the antiques store, and the neck of his guitar all rested there too.

"Were you ever in a band?"

"Me? No. Though we did sometimes play out with a

couple of friends. Just at coffee shops. In a record store once. Belinda sang. She had a pretty good voice."

"I remember that."

Sometimes, when they came for the holidays, he'd bring a guitar, and David played a little harmonica. But DJ didn't remember Elise as anything more than a cute kid, in the way that all kids can be—she hardly seemed like a kid to him now. "You play?"

She shook her head.

"I could show you a couple of chords, if you want."

"Maybe. I don't know. Not now, though."

"All right." Covering his disappointment, he turned his focus back to the figurine "I think I'm gonna let go now, have a smoke in the yard. But the offer stands."

She started to leave but turned back at the stairs. "Where will you put her?"

He looked around the basement, already full of her and Connie's things. "I really don't know."

DJ was still smoking in the yard when Connie appeared at the back door.

"I couldn't find you."

"I thought you were sleeping."

"I was. And then I wasn't."

She'd arranged to borrow a car for a week from a colleague whose wife was out of town and had turned up a couple of cars on Carfax, within fifty miles, each for around three thousand dollars. DJ had done some Googling of his own, found the Martin's resale value to be roughly the same, and tried not to think of the envelope of cash David had been waving about. There were still the records, but just getting to them seemed more trouble than they were worth. His heroic fantasy—any help he could really offer—a pathetic joke. Though it fell to him to do *something*.

"I could come up with that," he said. "But not right away."

"Meaning what exactly."

DJ flicked ash into the little pink bucket. "I could sell off one of my guitars, but it might take a while. They're still in Brooklyn, at Tracy's studio."

"Is there anything she didn't do for you? *Wait*," she said, and it was as if he could see her putting the pieces together. "Your records, your guitar—how much money do you have left?"

DJ exhaled a stream of smoke, a curtain of vapor that hung in the air. The money he'd frittered away was his own, but he wasn't much better off than David, standing in Ryan's driveway, saying *What's the point?*

"A negligible amount."

She repeated the phrase. "And your storage unit?"

"First and last and then..." He shrugged. What could he say that she'd want to hear? "Then I'd figure something out."

"Jesus Christ, DJ—that was your plan? I thought—I don't know what I thought. That you still had a *little* money left."

"I do," he said, meekly, unable to resist the opening. "It's just very little."

"Could you stop joking for once in your life? How do I surround myself with—"

"*Connie.* I'm not an idiot—I'm all too aware of what you're doing for me. I knew I'd have to at least get a part-time job—I just didn't know I was gonna have to do it this week." A bit of ash spilled out from the bucket as he stubbed out his cigarette against its side.

"Give me one of those, will you?"

"No."

"*No?*"

"All right, all right." He fished a cigarette from the pack and passed her his lighter.

She had to flick it a couple of times before the flame took hold, and DJ found the gesture uncanny in his sister's hands.

She took a deep drag and exhaled. "I used to filch your cigarettes—did you know that?"

"You did not."

She passed him the lighter. "Just a couple at a time."

"When was this?"

"That last summer, before you left for college. I'd just turned fourteen. Used to smoke them in the garage."

"*The garage.* How could you even get in there?" DJ lit a fresh cigarette. Their parents' garage had been packed with junk: broken appliances, bags of clothes that somehow never made it to Goodwill, half-empty cans of paint and varnish. And the place stank of gasoline. "I'm surprised you didn't blow yourself up."

"I seem to be doing that now. I haven't heard a peep from David—not that there's much he could say. I just thought, after last night...let me have that bucket." She put her cigarette out with self-disgust. "It still gives me a bad feeling—like what else could he be up to? It's too cold out here for me. Are you coming in?"

He held up his cigarette. "Soon as I finish this."

"Can I ask you something?"

"How can I still smoke?"

"Oh, no—I get that part. You stopped before and what good did it do you? I don't even want to know how you managed to run through a hundred thousand dollars with nothing to show for it. I just want to know why you'd get your friend to pack up all that stuff, why you'd spend the last of your money to move it up here, if you can't afford the storage. You let everything get trashed when it was still in your apartment. Why not just let it go?"

There'd been a minute, in the rental office when the clerk, a young woman barely out of high school, couldn't find his name. A minute in which his initial panic was overtaken by relief. Would he still grieve the loss of his and Belinda's belongings if—through no fault of his own—they'd simply disappeared? It wasn't so much that he wanted to see any of it again; it was that—until he'd seen it jammed ceiling-high in that storage space—it had been a comfort to know it would all be there.

DJ stubbed out his cigarette and set the bucket down by the door. "*Could you?*"

"No," she said. "Probably not. I just wouldn't have made someone else pack it."

"Fair enough."

She placed a hand on his back. "Well, my friend, you're going to have to do something about it now." Her phone rang and Connie reached into the back pocket of her jeans. "And now for the fun part," she said, and then, into the phone, "*Finally.*"

DJ had already stepped into the kitchen, wasn't sure what made him turn his head, but when he glanced back, she looked so mad it was as if her feet might lift off the ground.

"*Ryan.* You've got one hell of a … *No*—you listen to me. I'm in no mood. Just put him on." Connie leaned into the doorjamb, then closed her eyes. "Okay—stop, stop. Slow down. Where are you? Hang on—" All the color had drained from her face, but DJ could feel her mind working, her eyes now open and piercingly alert as she gave him instructions to get Elise, her bag, their coats. "I'm here. Mary's Avenue," she said into the phone, and then to DJ, "Go, go, go."

"What happened?" Elise said, lacing up her high tops as if this was nothing new.

"I'm not sure," DJ said. "Something with your dad."

"Is he okay?"

The best he could do by her was tell her the truth. "I don't know."

Connie was already behind the wheel, but still talking on the phone as they each got in.

"And Ryan?" she said. "When we get down there? I don't want to see you." She hung up, handed DJ her phone and started the car.

"Mom?" Elise leaned forward and Connie turned in her seat as she backed down the driveway.

"Your dad's okay. Concussion. Couple of cracked ribs. But he wrecked the truck."

Connie's bag sat at DJ's feet. He slid her phone into the side pocket, wished he'd thought to grab his own from the arm of couch where Elise had placed it while he was holding the glued figurine together. Tracy's call, unreturned; whatever message she might've left, unplayed.

He noticed, as if for the first time, that there never seemed to be anyone on the streets of Hurley, the yards manicured but vacant, the sky pale with a yellow cast behind the mesh of bare branches, the feel of evening coming on. In Brooklyn, at this time of day, he might be bothering to throw on something besides a ratty T-shirt and a pair of sweats, to walk down to the corner for more half-and-half, to the café that carried the French roast he favored, cigarettes from the Pakistani guy if he needed them. Some bit of air just to feel the world, walking past the familiar brownstone stoops, the cheap shops on Fifth Avenue he'd walked by with Belinda a million times, stopping in to pick up some little thing, a roll of scotch tape, of paper towel.

"Is he coming home with us?" said Elise.

DJ looked at Connie, startled by Elise's conclusion and the fact that she'd come to it. David strung out on pain meds, with no way to get home, and no one to care for him there. DJ hadn't wanted to ask Connie about what happened in the past, with Ryan, or Skip, or with David's using, but saw now that he should have; caught up in his own life, he'd given little thought to what hers had been like.

"Maybe for a night or two," she said. "I don't know."

Bed rest for the wicked? he was tempted to say, relieved David wasn't dead, that he hadn't run off, whether or not he'd been on his way. A dozen other quips bounced like pinballs off the bumpers of his brain, but for once DJ held his tongue. *Tilt*, he thought, *ding, ding, ding.*

7

Elise had had the wherewithal to bring her book, but DJ, stuck without his phone, took to going through his wallet. Only Connie was allowed in the ER itself, but DJ assumed that, in crisis mode, she'd wanted to herd them together. Or maybe she merely thought she'd need his help getting David in and out of the car. Either way, the waiting area was crowded, gurneys and wheelchairs coming and going, the hours they'd spent and those stretching before them having no discernible end.

From behind the leather card slots of his wallet, deep within the nylon fold, DJ pulled out a single frame cut from a photo-booth strip that showed him, Belinda, and Tracy mugging for the camera. They'd spent the afternoon knocking around the Lower East Side, the photo booth in a dive bar at the corner of 7th St. He'd saved it not because it was such a great shot—though it was—but because it had been such an ordinary weekend day, he and his wife and their cherished friend, unburdened by anything except deciding where to have dinner.

They'd each chosen one frame, Tracy taking the fourth as well, so she could pin it on the board in her studio, where he assumed it still hung with dozens of concert ticket stubs, Polaroids, and other ephemera. There were also the rolls of film Belinda had shot that day, prints and negatives buried somewhere in the mayhem behind the roll-up door at Catskill Park Storage. She'd never found a satisfying system to organize let alone catalogue her photographs. If that ever-growing collection was overwhelming for *her,* what on earth was he supposed to do?

"Can I see?" said Elise, and he brought the tiny image closer. "You guys look happy. Who's that?"

"That's Tracy."

"Your friend who helped you move?"

"You don't miss a beat."

"I remember Belinda taking a lot of pictures. One of those cameras with a really big lens."

"A Pentax. That's right." He thought he should say something about David, only he couldn't think what. "I saw a candy machine in the hall. You want a Snickers or something?"

"I think it's just soda."

"Better than nothing." He stood up, stretched his back, and then there was Connie.

"You going somewhere?"

"Just to the soda machine."

"They're bringing him out in a minute. God, my feet are killing me."

"Are you all right?" asked DJ. "Is he?"

"Go ahead—you got time. You could get me a water. I'm fine. And he will be." She plunked down next to Elise. "How about you, bunny?"

Elise shrugged and bent her forehead toward Connie's. DJ found it hard to turn away. Just the water boy, he thought, but then Connie glanced up at him with an affection that left him tearful as he moved down the dreary hall, the soda machine like a beacon before him. He would bring her all the water in the world.

Having fallen asleep in his clothes, DJ pulled fresh ones from the plastic drawers, went upstairs, and took a long hot shower. When he came out of the bathroom, Connie and Elise's doors were still shut, David snoring lightly on the living room sofa, huddled under an afghan. DJ measured out grounds for a full pot of coffee and set it to brew. Then he scouted around in Connie's cabinets for flour, sugar, and baking powder, held up a small bottle of vanilla with a whispered *yes!* He set a pan out on the stove, a stack of plates on the counter, mixed the ingredients for pancakes into separate bowls, wet and dry, and proudly poured himself a steaming cup of coffee.

"Hey, Deej?" David called softly. "Is that you?"

DJ came to the doorway. "How could you tell?"

"Connie wouldn't be that quiet. I gotta ask you a favor, old man. Can you help me sit up?"

The night before, it had taken both him and Connie to get David out of the hospital wheelchair and settled into the front seat. DJ set his coffee down beside the bottle of pills on the dining table. David had been in a fog when they brought him home; now he seemed clear-eyed but wincing as he moved the top half of the crocheted blanket aside.

"What should I do?"

"Just take some of the weight—yeah, my shoulder— that's good. Now brace me." Using only his legs, David sidled over so he could rest his forearm on the pillow, an oddly intimate moment, all of his bravado and scrappy charm set aside. Just a man, adrift on his ex-wife's sofa, with broken ribs.

"How many?" said DJ, patting his own ribcage.

"Three." David glanced at the pills. "You still have that thing about fours?"

"Yeah—I do." The number had always given him an uneasy feeling, something hauntingly off kilter despite its evenness.

"You wanna pass me those?"

DJ wasn't about to dispense so much as an aspirin to David. "You should wait for Connie."

David brought his hands gingerly to his face, a band of

bruising below his eyes. "The other day … I shouldn't have dragged you along. I don't know what I was thinking. Is Elise—did I see Elise last night?"

"Why don't I bring you some coffee." There were so many things DJ wanted to ask—about the money, the house, why he'd bothered to lie—but David looked sadder than he'd ever seen him, and DJ didn't want to be caught between him and Connie again. He started toward the kitchen, but David said, "What were you fussing with in there?"

"I was going to make pancakes. Once everyone was up."

"Well look at you, Martha Stewart—*ow*." There was a crackle of static as David tried to pull the resistant afghan across his knees. "Milk," he said. "Please. And a little sugar."

"*It's a good thing*," DJ let the reference play before he added, "that she still cares."

"God, my head hurts." Cradling his ribs with one arm, David raised the other just far enough to press the base of his palm against his forehead. He closed his eyes and let out a long sigh.

He'd swerved right to avoid a sinkhole—was the story Ryan told Connie—and then, to avoid an oncoming car, swerved so hard to the left that despite his best efforts to steer, his flooring the brakes, he'd hit the back corner of a double-parked UPS truck. David's side had borne the brunt of the impact, and neither Ryan, nor the UPS driver safely wheeling a hand truck full of cartons up the street, had gotten hurt. Like a recounted dream, to DJ it rang more of allegory than fact—though David's injuries and his damaged truck were indisputable. Whether the story was entirely true was unclear; what they were up to and where they were going left out.

David settled his arm back on the pillow. "It's easy enough to get on her bad side, but no side at all? I don't think that's possible. Do you?"

"Not unless you're Ryan." DJ thought of all the people he'd shunned in his life, of those who—in one way or another—had shut him out. Then he went into the kitchen and fixed a cup of coffee for David.

From the hall that led to the bathroom and two small bedrooms, you could also enter Connie's living room; the common areas of her house all had open doorways. It wasn't long before she passed through with a gruff *good morning*, then returned from the kitchen with a cup of coffee of her own, Elise marking the same circular path shortly after, but with a glass of orange juice. It was as though each of them had agreed—that at least for breakfast—there should be a reprieve. DJ made pancakes and Elise ferried them in, everyone worn out and polite as they sent the butter and maple syrup around, David set up with an old TV tray, another remnant from their parents' house. Connie wasn't much better at letting go of things—just neater.

"Hidden away in the laundry room," she said. "I don't know why I didn't think of it for you. You can have it when," she'd started to say, then trailed off, the undetermined length of David's stay, and her reference to it, hanging in the air. "Well," she said, taking up a big forkful of pancakes, "these are really good. Better than mine. What's your secret?"

DJ made a brief show of it, as if he wasn't going to tell, before giving in. "A little vanilla."

Vanilla, everyone murmured, no one ready to let the morning's peace go.

DJ was enjoying a post-breakfast cigarette and Connie had come out to tell him she was going for a walk, though she was slow to leave.

"You know the ironic thing?" she said. "Now he's going to be living in that house for free for who knows how long before the bank actually evicts him."

"Do you wish you'd stayed?"

"No. Maybe. I don't know." She looked around at the scraggly patch of yard, cordoned off from the plot of woods behind it by a low weathered fence. "Which is the thread you can pull without unraveling the rest? What's that Ray Bradbury story?"

"The one where they don't let the little girl see the sun?"

"*No.*"

DJ laughed. "The one where the guy travels back in time to hunt T. rex and haplessly alters the course of history."

"Because he steps on a *butterfly*."

"'A Sound of Thunder'."

"A fucking butterfly. What I wish," she said, "is that he could've stayed clean. Never gone off the deep end, never made it more than a casual thing. Who do you know that didn't do any coke back in the day? Even his loyalty to his stupid friends—would I really undo that part of what makes him who he is?"

DJ blew a stream of smoke up into the bare trees. After breakfast, they'd had to help David up and down from the couch, but he'd been able to make his own way to the bathroom, and DJ hoped to God he wouldn't stay more than a couple of days.

"It's like this tantalizing ritual," she went on. "A deep indulgence, and a taste, a *desire,* for something grand. He was always–well, *you* know. Charming. He was always fun."

She looked at him for confirmation, and DJ nodded, let her keep reasoning it out.

"And he's good with Elise. Or he can be when he's actually present. Which he had been, for a good long while—despite our differences." Connie looked back at the house, the small house whose tranquility DJ, and now David, had invaded. "How could he be so fucking careless? I wish we still had the damn house to sell. That I hadn't trusted him. So stupid, right? And now he's in there with broken ribs. What was I supposed to do? Leave him with Ryan?"

"*Connie,*" DJ tried to say, but she just mowed on.

"He was trying, and I wanted to believe it could all work out. Not my marriage, but the rest of it—yeah. I wanted to believe that he'd be all right. If something worse had happened…" The look she gave him now was like a plea, then she shook it off. "But no—to answer your question. I don't wish that I'd stayed in the house."

What DJ could see was that Connie needed someone to talk to, that maybe this, more than anything else, was why she'd let him move in. But it was hard to hear these things and not feel cast in equivalent guilt. David's misdeeds might be on a larger scale, but there were so many ways, especially around work and money, that—throughout his marriage—he'd let Belinda down. DJ knew Connie's reference to David's loyalty wasn't meant as a dig but felt it anyway. And what he heard, running beneath it all, was a painful truth. No matter how disappointed or angry she might be or become, no matter how certain she was that they couldn't—that she didn't want to—"work it out," Connie still did, and would probably always, love David. It was a fucked-up world, love an impossible thing—what could you make of your life?

If you had a kid, if you'd raised a good kid like Elise, you'd at least accomplished something. Then all you had to do was hope that the world—or you, yourself—didn't crush her.

One of the best photos Belinda ever took was a shot of her nephews, two towheaded boys, raised in the small Indiana town where she grew up. A sepia print showed them grinning and twin-like though a year apart, barefoot in frayed denim shorts and cartoon-blazoned T-shirts, behind them a field of tall grass bending in the wind. A junior and senior in high school the year she died, they'd appeared gangling and self-conscious in dark grown-up suits at the memorial, their pained confusion impossible to face. Elise must've been there too, but DJ had no image of her. Neither he nor Belinda had wanted kids, which precluded the question of their handling that responsibility. And neither did he—nor, he imagined, anyone else—hold regrets on that account. Even Connie, manager of all things, was only stumbling through. They were none of them exempt from making a mess of their lives. Look who she was forced to turn to.

DJ put out his cigarette, followed her back into the kitchen and then out again through the side door that led to the carport, where he dumped his small bucketful of ashes into the huge rubber garbage can. "You want me to come with you? I could use a good ramble."

Connie tipped her head toward the house. "I'd feel better if you stayed. His pain meds are on my dresser now—but he's not due for another two hours."

"Sure," he said, though it didn't seem to satisfy her.

"Did I ever tell you that before we were married, before we were even dating, when I got pregnant with Mark? You remember Mark."

"I guess." DJ remembered that she'd found herself pregnant by a guy who she'd only just learned had been cheating on her.

"Anyway. It was David who drove me to Planned Parenthood. He drove me, and then he waited for me in that hideous clinic, held my hand in his brand-new Camry afterwards, until I'd finally stopped crying. I'm just saying."

"Right." DJ watched her walk down the driveway. As she neared the bottom, without turning around, she gave him one of Elise's little backhanded waves.

While Connie was out, Elise brought up a stack of board games from the basement. Life. Monopoly. Risk. Sorry. Who thought up these things? David flashed him a look, and DJ nodded. Despite the house and whatever else

David had or hadn't done, he and DJ would do this, they'd play nice for Elise—it was easy enough to fall back on their usual repartee.

After an inconclusive debate over which game to play, she went back to the basement and returned with a jigsaw puzzle. A small solid purple circle that once assembled, she insisted, would fit, if just barely, the TV tray.

DJ and Elise each brought a dining chair close to the couch, the little table centered between the three of them. With the box on her lap, she sifted through, searching for the rounded edge pieces, as DJ and David one-upped each other with lyrics and song titles—"Purple Haze," "Will It Go Round in Circles"—Elise giving her game-show buzz to those too punny or too much of a stretch. It was still early, a sunny spring afternoon, but DJ had that Sunday night sense of dread he'd had as a kid, clinging to each fragile minute of weekend freedom before Monday set in.

They finished the puzzle, but Connie hadn't returned, and DJ, still seated in the hard-backed chair, following a chain of musical Googling set off by their lyric match, couldn't help exchanging another glance with David, who made a quiet aside. "She—of all people—would call if anything was awry."

In the same half-whisper, DJ said, "Unless."

"*I'm right here,*" said Elise. She'd settled with her book in the upholstered armchair across from the couch. "And she's been gone for almost two hours—if anyone's keeping track."

"You want to call?" David said to DJ. "Or should I?"

Only Elise faced the set of windows that looked onto the street. With a finger holding her place in her closed book, she leaned forward in the chair. "Someone's pulling into the driveway. A white car."

"Shit—*ow,*" said David, turning to see.

DJ stood to get a better view. "Please tell me you don't know whose car that is."

"You want to take it easy there, *Deej?*" David said, with a sneer. "Because I don't. And you've got no business—you've got no place."

"Oh, *that's* rich."

"*Stop*," said Elise, who'd come up to the window and stood beside DJ. "It's just Mom."

"Like anyone I know would drive a Ford Focus," David muttered, as they all settled back into their previous positions.

Having entered the house through the kitchen, Connie now stood in the doorway to the living room, the color high in her cheeks, a plastic grocery bag in her hand. "Hey Lisey," she said. Then looking from DJ to David, "What's happening here?"

"Nothing," they said in near unison.

"You know what?" she said. "I'm just goonna leave that one alone." She held up the plastic bag. "I brought you some clothes."

"*Shit,*" said David. "Thanks."

"Whose car is that?" said Elise.

"A nurse on the unit. His wife's. I was already out walking—figured I'd save us the trouble—their house was just further than I thought." She sat down on the arm of Elise's chair, worked a key off her ring. "You'll take mine, Deej. One less thing for me to worry about."

David smirked at him, and DJ said, "Kettle black."

Connie looked to Elise, who opened her book and said, "I think they need a time out."

"Who of us doesn't," said Connie, then she walked down the hall to her room.

The clinking of forks marked the growing silence as they made their way through bowls of spaghetti and jarred sauce. After dinner, Elise disassembled the puzzle and DJ carried the box with him to the basement. He tucked the puzzle in with the games, then took all the books out of a central, eye-height row, and rearranged them in vertical stacks. This cleared a small space where he could fit Belinda's figurine.

DJ felt better, but compelled to do more, to make the place his own. Regardless of the circumstances that brought him, he had more of a right to be here, in Connie's house, than David, having only wrecked his *own* life—and not hers.

When he'd unpacked, he buried the bright Kodak box of photos beneath his clothes, in the bottommost plastic drawer. Now he brought it back out and gently laid it on one end of the coffee table. DJ settled on the couch, lifted the yellow lid, and placed it face down. He took a deep breath, and then, pulling against the light suction, the soft shush of black cardboard, he opened the interior box.

The photo he was after was an eight-by-ten, a black-and-white portrait of Belinda, taken and printed by her college roommate, the fixer in the lower left corner faded to near white. For years it had been hidden, randomly or deliberately tucked away in a copy of Bruce Davidson's *Brooklyn Gang* but had tumbled out and then been carried down the long hall to the bedroom of his apartment by a friend of Tracy's. A woman he didn't know—she must have it bad for Tracy to wade into his move.

Apparently, she'd knocked, though he hadn't heard it through noise-canceling headphones and was duly startled when she entered his bedroom. A lithe black woman whose stunning good looks overshadowed the young woman in the print she held before him. She named the book, wanting to know if she should tuck it back in, and DJ reached up, took the photo from her hand, and silently lay it beside him on the bed.

"She was lovely," the woman said, then left, gently closing the door behind her.

In the photo, thin loose curls frame Belinda's face, sunlight cutting across it. She's standing in a doorway, her head tilted to one side, her smile one of clear affection for the photographer. The kind of shot that can only be taken by someone who really knows you. The Belinda he'd first met all those years ago.

There were others in the box, Polaroids and snapshots of Belinda, the two of them together or with friends, and a few of her finest prints. But there was a frankness to this one that drew you in.

He closed the inner box, replaced the gaudy lid. Then he brought the photo over to Connie's shelves and leaned it against one of the pillar-like stacks of books he'd made on either side of the dancing figurine. It slid down at first, the glossy paper lightweight, but after a few tries he found the proper angle to keep it standing.

Monday morning it rained and rained, water blearing the windows, coursing down the driveway, the slate path, like the tributaries of a river. Out back, DJ smoked under the eave, bits of straw-like grass rising here and there above the sheet of water covering the yard.

"It's like Noah's ark up here," he said to Tracy, having finally returned her call. Then he filled her in on all that had happened, ending with his idea to sell off the guitar.

"The Martin? Oh, DJ—I'm sorry. When are you coming down?"

"That's the thing—I don't see how I can. I was hoping you could ship it." He paused, knowing she would do it if he asked, but regretting it just the same. "Or maybe sell it for me?"

There was silence on her end of the line. "I've been stalling, but as long as it's one big shit-show, I may as well tell you now. I'm selling the studio."

"You are not."

"I think I have to—it's been a slow year, and the offer's too good. I'm gonna sell, then I'm gonna go out to L.A. for a while."

DJ felt a sickening loss of equilibrium. Tracy had worked in L.A. before, talked of moving there someday, but she was a talented sound engineer with a boutique studio in Williamsburg, and he'd not taken her musings seriously. "Well, that explains it."

"Explains what?"

"Why you'd ship me off," he said, trying to make a joke of it, but it didn't play.

"I shipped your *stuff*, but I didn't ship you. You had no money and no apartment. Where were you gonna go?"

Your place now, he couldn't help thinking, though of course she would sublet for more than her already high rent, and he wasn't about to tell her the disastrous ending to her packing saga. Somewhere in that mess out on Route 28 was the ukulele she'd given him, and that, in and of itself, was breaking his heart. He was a terrible friend. "Why didn't you tell me you were thinking about this?"

"I didn't really think it would *happen*, for one thing—I turned down the first offer they made—and for another, you don't think you're just a little out of line? I mean, I knew it would be a shock. But I thought, oh—you know— that you might be *happy* for me. It wasn't like I was ever seeing your sequestered ass until you had to move. You can still take your sweet time to return my calls when I'm out in California."

"I am happy for you," he said, but they could both hear how thin it sounded. "At least I want to be."

At this she laughed. "It's a tough situation—even if you did put yourself there. When it rains…"

I think I'll miss you most of all, he wanted to say, Dorothy's line to the Scarecrow, but said only "Don't even."

"I can sell the Martin for you, if you're sure. What do you want to do about the rest?"

A gust of wind sent a curtain of rain across his legs, and he had an idea. "Could you send me the Yamaha? I'd like to give it to Elise. And then sell the others. Don't you have a guy at Sam Ash? Whatever you can get. I could use the money." He'd make a lot more if he sold them on Craigslist one by one, but he wasn't about to have her send a dozen guitars up to Connie's. And even if he did, it would just be that much harder to see them go.

"This is not what we pictured for our lives, is it," she said, and it seemed impossible to think she'd once slept curled beside him in his Brooklyn bed. "Maybe I can shoot up there for an afternoon before I go."

"So it's definite then."

"I think so. And the beautiful Martin?"

"Yes, ma'am."

"All right. I know someone who might want her—get you good dollar for that. Something fair-ish from my guy for the rest. Let me talk to you in a couple of days."

"*Sayonara*," he said.

"*Au revoir.*"

After she hung up, DJ smoked the last cigarette in his pack. Then he stepped out from beneath the eave and let the rain soak him through.

Having changed and towel-dried his hair, DJ felt obliged to check in on David before leaving, but David was either asleep or pretending to be—which was just fine with him. DJ had his own agenda and a couple of hours before he had to pick up Elise.

He parked across from the antiques store; the rain tapered to a drizzle. A foolish fantasy, he supposed—that she'd close up shop for lunch, that he'd bring something in. She did say she was chained to the store. *A distraction*, Connie would say, but he wanted—he needed—something to hope for, no matter how unlikely the odds.

He ducked under the permanent canopy, the rhythm of his heart picking up, but the door didn't give. The movable clock hands of the be-back-by sign were set to eleven, which it was long past. Only looking closer did he note the daily hours which said closed on Mondays—like everything else in this tourist driven town. He placed his hand on the glass-paneled door and peered in, just able to make out a bent figure, dragging a box from behind the counter out into the aisle. With a pleasurable jangle of nerves, he gave the door the loud first half of a shave and a haircut knock. The figure straightened. Not Andrea, but a man—the Post-it wielding brother. *Alex*—that was it—crossed his hands like a ref calling out a bad play. DJ held up a finger, signing just one minute. Alex shook his head no, but DJ recognized that dragging of a heavy box, would've bet his life that what it contained was records. Andrea had made him sound like a difficult man, but maybe Alex could help him. He put his hands together, as if to say please, and though Alex splayed his own in exasperation, he came and opened the door.

"You must be Alex."

"Must I?"

The deflection threw him, but DJ said his own name and extended his hand. Alex didn't take it.

"Friday afternoon's the first opening I've got for an appraisal—most people call."

DJ followed partway as Alex sidestepped the box, bypassing the counter to switch on the overhead lights. He pulled an appointment book from beside the register and flipped through its pages.

"Saturdays are good, Sundays better, if it's a full estate. Can I ask who referred you?"

The box, DJ could see now, was filled with old ledgers, but he remained undeterred. "It's not an estate, actually."

The look Alex gave him was one of strained patience. "No?"

"Your sister—Andrea—I stopped in here last week." Once again, he extended his hand, this time toward the counter display. "I bought the marbled glass egg?"

"Well, whatever you bought, she should've told you all sales are final."

"No—I love the egg. A present," he said, fumbling on, "for my niece. She loved the egg." DJ felt his dignity slipping farther and farther away, wished he could stop saying *egg*.

"My sister is well-intentioned. But she's a little flighty." Alex set the appointment book back in its spot. "Was there something else I can help you with?"

"I have a collection of records," he started to say, but Alex cut him off.

"Right there on the table," he said, pointing toward the crate of 78s and classical records DJ had noted the first time he came in. "Already more than I want."

"I hear that. But I was hoping you could refer me to a dealer."

"Ah," said Alex. "I might know someone. What kind of a collection are we talking about? Did you bring a list?"

"I wasn't—I hadn't planned," DJ stammered and felt his cheeks flush. He'd imagined the cartons and crates lined up before the rows of green doors, someone counting bills out into his hand and taking away the whole lot. He probably knew half of what he had but would be hard-pressed to literally recount it. "I don't have a list."

Alex studied him, his general air of irritation giving way to a knowing sympathy. "You were looking for Andrea."

"I was."

"But you do have records—a serious collection?"

"I do."

From the counter, Alex picked up a business card for the store and wrote a number on the back. "I can make a couple of calls. Try me tomorrow at the end of business. And if you make a deal..."

"You'll take a piece."

"A small one. Ten percent?"

"I can live with that."

"Very good," said Alex, and they shook hands now, the box of old ledgers between them.

DJ was halfway to the door when Alex said his name, as though trying it on. "Was that something you used to do?"

Used to—DJ couldn't fault the conclusion. At this age, with his woodsman-like beard, someone might guess him a musician, but no one would peg him as a deejay. "Coincidental, though I've spun a few."

"I wouldn't get my hopes up," said Alex.

"Whatever you can do," DJ said, though he knew Alex didn't mean the records.

Now all he had to do was figure a way to dig them out.

Even with stopping for gas, DJ arrived at Elise's school ahead of schedule. But a heavier rain had resumed, and he found himself farther back in the pick-up line than ever. For a solid half hour after his exchange with Alex, DJ had felt good, and then, as with everything else, his confidence faded, the consequences of impulsive choices looming. How *would* he get his records out from beneath that pile? And after that? After however much cash he ended up getting for them and his guitars—what then? Like the money from Belinda's insurance, it too would run out. He might as well give whatever he garnered to Connie, put it toward what she owed Gretchen and Denise. Then it would mean something to her at least, all his indulgent spending, all the hours across the years that he'd idled away in record stores.

From the minute he'd boarded that first bus to Kingston, it was as if he'd been jumping bizarre and contentious hurdles, new ones rising with each one he cleared. A grand fuss beyond which the days stretched out blankly before him. He dreaded going back to work, and yet he would have to. Elise was a great kid, as far as kids went, and were the question put bluntly to him, he couldn't deny she'd already won a place in his heart. But could he really be tied down to her daily care? To have his freedom curtailed was to lose it. He'd stepped boldly forward and now he'd have to keep his word, when the only thing he wanted to do was lie down. Every job he'd ever worked had some association to failure or loss. Quitting, after all, was the thing he did best. An Olympian quitter—and disappointer—medals bronze, silver, and gold. Elise might like him, but he was only her uncle, a man she hardly knew, and she'd not signed up to be tied to him either, which seemed clear enough when she raised her hand in stoic greeting, a small flowered umbrella bobbing above her head as she raced to the car.

DJ reached across the front seat, his neck pinching as he flicked the handle, then threatening to spasm as he stretched his hand to push open the door.

"Hi ho," he managed to get out before pulling back and digging his fingers into the pain.

She tossed her umbrella into the back and climbed in, gently shutting the door, Connie's Civic not requiring the force of David's Camry.

"Hey," she said, the word a fatigued exhale, then shoved her backpack to the floor and buckled up. "Okay, ready," she said, and he answered *Rightio,* but all they could do was inch forward in the line, the rain battering down on the roof, sluicing along the windshield.

"Whoa!" they both said, at a flash of lightning, their eyes wide as they met, thunder rumbling up and rolling over them.

"Nice day for ducks," he said.

"For otters."

"For narwhals."

"Narwhals?" she said.

"Unicorn of the sea." He put on the blinker, though it was too soon to turn.

"For *hippopotami*," she said.

He chuckled. "That's good. Very good."

Elise rested her head back and let out a sigh, as though whatever ills or drudgery of the school day had slipped behind her, and DJ wanted to do whatever he could to make the moment last.

"Should we pick something up? Fries from the diner? Or we could sit down for a piece of pie."

"Too greasy," she said. "Too much."

"A head of lettuce then."

"Can we just go home?"

A crossing guard had stopped the line a few cars up, where a regiment of kids, some with billowing umbrellas, others with their heads bowed beneath the hoods of their slickers, traipsed over to the waiting buses, and DJ could, for the first time, see Connie's point.

"Sure," he said. "If that's what you want."

"Is my dad still at the house?"

DJ hesitated. Nothing had been said of how long David would or wouldn't stay, and he tried to think what it would be like if the man he'd left huddled in Connie's living room were his father. "As far as I know."

She nodded, as though this both was and wasn't an answer to the question she'd asked. Then the crossing guard blew her whistle and waved them on.

"*Hey*," said Elise. "You said we could go home."

Before he'd given it real thought, DJ had driven in the opposite direction.

"Just a little detour." It was the last thing he wanted, but it was a thing he could do. He'd fill out an application at the Barnes & Noble across from the mall, and if there was an opening, even as a cashier, he would take it.

"*Hey, Deej?*" David called out as he and Elise came in through the kitchen door. "Guy left a package out front."

"In the rain," DJ said.

"What's eating him?" said David, from in his spot on the couch. "It's hard enough to get up by myself, I couldn't have bent down to get it anyway. You wanna sit?"

Elise hesitated, then—citing too much homework—said she'd take a snack to her room.

In spite of himself, DJ felt a little pang for David. He knew she preferred doing her homework at the living room table, suspected a variety of conflicted emotions had directed her choice.

DJ opened the front door and the package, left leaning against it, fell forward onto the sopping slate. He swept it up—the record player he'd ordered for Connie—and ducked back inside.

"Whaddya got?" called David. "I hope you're talking to me, because I'm bored out of my mind. You go out—you don't even leave me a note?"

DJ stared at him from the front hall. "You gotta be kidding me."

"Have to be, wouldn't I? Having strained your *affection*."

"Among other things."

"You gonna open that?"

"It's a gift," said DJ. "For Connie."

David struggled to shift back on the cushion. "Christ—you'd think they'd give you a brace."

Droplets of rain clung to the packing tape. DJ brushed them off. "It's a record player—for her 45s."

"Sentimental."

"Most good presents are." The manager at the Barnes & Noble wouldn't even let him fill out an application, claimed he already had more than he knew what to do with, and though Elise had once again perused the graphic novels, she refused to let him buy her one. All he wanted now was to go down to the basement. Play some guitar. Try to finish his composition. Having David in the house was a royal pain in the ass. But something expectant in his demeanor held DJ in place.

"Listen, Deej. Another day, maybe two, and I can take care of myself. But I don't want to go back to the house." He carefully raised an arm, pressed his fingers to his temple. "Connie's set up a meeting with the lawyer for Thursday so we can...whatever that word is—finalize. And I've been sitting here on her couch all afternoon with a headache and too much time to think. I don't have the money to fix the truck and they're going to suspend my license, anyway. I just want to know if you plan on sticking around."

DJ set the box on the dining table. "Because you're not."

As though gauging their tenderness, David touched his ribs. "I've got a cousin in Silver Spring. I can do drywall for him once these babies heal up. Four months' suspension and a thousand dollar fine. I have to clean up, and I can't do it here, in fucking Hurley."

"And Connie knows this?"

"I'm telling her tonight. I just wanted...she's gonna need your help, and Elise...well, Elise is already mad. But she likes you—anyone can see that."

David's hair was matted, his face pale and his eyes red-rimmed. He seemed in genuine pain, and DJ had a queasy feeling of being pulled down. "What about *you*?"

"Be better for both of them if I'm not around like some constant reminder of everything I screwed up. Just a couple of months, till I get myself together. I already signed over the pink slip, but maybe I can get you back the car."

"Jesus, David."

"I know—and I don't believe in those things. But this accident? It really feels like a sign. I mean, *the house*—I know what you think—how reckless can I be? Except the bank—those guys are vultures. I had most of the money. You saw. I would've gotten the rest." He closed his eyes and lay his head back. "Or maybe not. What a fucking mess. My father was dead when I was her age. At least she's got that going for her, even if I'm down in Maryland for a while."

Tempted to make Elise's buzzer sound, DJ said, "It's your life. I'm hardly the one to advise." As he moved toward the fireplace, David raised his head.

"But you'll be here."

On one end of Connie's mantel a silver frame held a winter photograph. David with a young Elise in his arms, Connie leaning into him, her smile wide, all of them wearing Santa hats. A thick acrylic frame displayed a colorful shot of Gretchen and Denise, along with their husbands, on what looked to be a recent island or Florida vacation. DJ picked up a small wooden frame with a black-and-white photo of the four of them as kids. In the backyard of their parents' house, they formed a staggered line, DJ a skinny and strange being among them. He set the photo down and turned back to David. "Certainly looks that way."

For dinner, DJ made them all fines herbes omelets—courtesy of Jacques Pépin—no easy task in Connie's clumsy pans. But the meal had blown up, Elise leaving the table without saying a word once David announced his plans. DJ tried to bolt too, but Connie had reached for his arm and said, "*No*—you stay." So he'd sat in his place as the two of them argued on and on about what was best, Connie deploying the full range of her persuasive abilities, insisting she could get him into a good program here.

"I'm not going to *rehab*," David all but shouted, "and I don't want you doing anything more for me. I'm grateful,

Connie, I am—but it's enough. You of all people should see that. It's better this way."

"Not for her," she said.

"That's a matter of opinion." David struggled to standing and moved back to the couch—the closest he could come to storming out—and neither Connie nor DJ helped him.

"When are you leaving then?" she finally said.

"Friday morning. There's a Greyhound at eight something."

"So, I'm supposed to drop you, is that it?"

"Or I can take a cab." He looked at DJ. "Maybe you could take me by the house before then, help me pick up some stuff? Another day and I should be able to manage the stairs."

DJ looked to Connie, who looked back at him, resigned. "You might as well. Nothing *I* say is gonna make a difference, is it?"

"No," said David. "It's not."

Connie's chair screeched as she pushed back from the table. "I'm going to go talk to her. Then I'll come back and clear."

"I'll do it," said DJ.

"You cooked—I'll do it."

"I'll live. Go talk to her."

"*Fine*," she said. "Fine."

DJ gathered up silverware and stacked plates.

"That went well," David said.

DJ's back was turned to him, but he could feel David's agitation. "What did you think she would say?"

"Don't let the door hit you on the way out?"

DJ picked up the plates. "She doesn't much care for any plan that's not her own."

"How'd you and Belinda work it out?"

The question rocked him, made him turn around.

"Seriously," David said. "I'm asking. Because this—this now?" He winced, trying to shift his position. "This is all

107

my doing. The coke, the house—I get that. But it's like…
what—I don't know. More blood under the bridge. I know
things weren't always so hunky-dory with the two of you—
half the time you didn't even have a job."

DJ just stood there, a pile of dirty dishes in his hands,
Elise's barely touched omelet on top. "That's not how it
was." For a second, he'd thought David was referring to
Sarah, though there was no way he'd know about her.

"So maybe not *half*, but you know what I'm saying."

"You could stay." It was what he'd done, wasn't it? Even
when he'd imagined leaving Belinda was what he wanted,
he hadn't been able to do it—and the situations were hardly
the same. He'd had to wonder sometimes, why she hadn't
left him, which he supposed was David's point. Even without a kid to tie them, he and Belinda had been bound in a
more permanent way. *Till death do you part.*

"Growing up," said David, "I never imagined I'd get married, let alone have a kid. But then I met Connie, and I was a
better person with her—much to everyone's surprise. I'm not
blind, you know? And for a while, I really thought I could
change. Kidded myself that I had. We had Elise. I went into
business for myself. I even let you beat me at ping-pong."

"Hey, now—"

"But water seeks its own level, right? Or some other
stupid bullshit. No one really changes. You think it'd be
any better if I stayed? I'd just go on breaking their hearts."

"Or someone's heart, anyway."

"Don't get all *perceptive* on me, Deej."

His hands ached from holding the plates, but he stood
his ground. "I miss that guy."

David closed his eyes and settled back. "You and me both."

Retreating to the basement, DJ opened his iPad, saved
a fresh version of the audio file for his unfinished com-

position with its troublesome melody. For the joke and lack of anything better, he'd named it Old_Unresolved, but too rattled to make any progress, he soon took off his headphones, relieved to hear Connie's footsteps on the stairs.

"Nice," she said of his changes to her shelves. "She looks good there. Your statuette. Did you do that just now?"

"This morning."

She perched on the arm of the couch, and DJ was caught between wanting to say something about David and not knowing what to say. Rather than any trite or misguided attempt at sympathy, he said, "Do you ever just sit down anywhere?"

"What do you mean? I'm sitting now. If I slide over onto your sofa there, I might never get up." Connie yawned and rubbed her face, then let her chin rest in her hands. "I've been going over and over this in my head, and I can't have you buying a car just so you can pick my kid up from school."

"If you say." Comfortably riding around in her old Civic, hustling to sell off his things, he'd somehow lost track of the idea that the bulk of the money was meant for a car.

"Even if we split the price," she went on, "there'd still be gas and maintenance—not to mention insurance. I'll take her to school, but if you could see your way to being here when she gets home, then she can take the bus. Once I return the Focus, she'll have to."

DJ was oddly disappointed; he liked driving Elise.

"It'll limit your job options though."

"My plethora of options."

"*Yeah*," she said, a conceding half-laugh. "But it's a worthier contribution. If I hired some college kid, it'd be zero sum."

Andrea had used the same expression. He should get it tattooed on his forehead. "David said he'd try to get the Camry back."

"*Really*," said Connie, and DJ wished he hadn't mentioned his name, let alone anything David said he'd try to do.

"Well," she said. "I wouldn't count on that. Though it'd certainly make things easier."

Neither of them spoke. DJ thought of the record player, still sitting in its Amazon box upstairs. He could go up and get it or he could ask the question running in the back of his mind since the day he arrived.

"What would you do if I wasn't here?"

"Are you saying I should be grateful?"

"*No.* No—I was just thinking how strange it is. If you were sorry you'd taken me in."

"If you weren't here?" She slid over on the couch beside him. "I suppose I'd rent out the basement—my original plan. For less now, though, with no second bathroom. To a med student or a nurse who works twelve-hour shifts—someone who wouldn't be around much, except to sleep. And Elise would have to spend five miserable afternoons a week in the after-school program."

"You *have* been going over this."

"I'm taking Thursday off to see the lawyer. Think I'll take Friday, too."

"You should. You deserve it."

"Yeah, yeah—not so fast. While we have the two cars, we should see what we can do about your storage."

"Better to think about my stuff than yours?"

"You're gonna have to face it sometime."

"I know."

"And I said I'd help you. That's not going to change just because," she swept her hand toward the ceiling, but didn't go on.

DJ could tell her about Alex, about Tracy selling his guitars, but he didn't want it to be something he was *trying*. He wanted to wait till those potentialities were definite; he wanted to show her that he could come through.

"That's a good shot of her," Connie said, then she went upstairs.

Captive only to his own desires these last years alone, DJ had lapsed into a lack of routine, could not have imagined himself hostage to this ever-growing regime of obligation. A trial he didn't know if he could survive. But the next morning, everyone on good behavior, conversation kept within a neutral zone, the day had ground on as planned, with him its unlikely captain.

As afternoon faded, Elise was doing homework in her room, David reading on the couch. She was barely speaking to him, but she'd deigned to bring him a stack of books from the basement, including DJ's old copy of *Catcher in the Rye*. On the title page, his name had been crossed out, Connie's written in her tidy script beneath it. DJ stepped out into the yard for a cigarette, then called the number on the back of Alex's card.

"Alex's phone," a woman answered after several rings. *Andrea.*

"This is DJ."

"Hey! We're at the hospital. A baby girl! Seven and a half pounds, all fingers and toes accounted for. Hang on."

He thought she was going to put Alex on, but she'd just moved into the hall. "Rough labor. His wife—Molly— she's not doing so well."

"*Oh*," said DJ, "sorry."

"Yeah. She keeps wanting him to take the baby. *Alicia.* Pretty, right?"

"It is—congratulations." So much for Alex making any calls. Just as he was thinking it a good thing he hadn't mentioned it to Connie, Andrea said, "I hear you're selling some records."

"Trying to."

"He wanted to know if I thought you were a stand-up guy. You got any Dusty Springfield?"

"Probably."

On pitch, in a light clear voice, she sang the swinging melody of "You Don't Have to Say You Love Me" into the phone. "I've still got a turntable at my place in Brooklyn. Maybe I can take a look at what you've got before you divest."

DJ's head spun. Alex had asked her about him? She had a turntable? And then the kicker. "Your place in Brooklyn?"

"Park Slope. I'm just staying up here for a while, helping Alex out—much to Molly's dismay. You would think—hold on a sec." *It's DJ,* he heard her say, but couldn't make out the rest. *Park Slope.* It was like a lens coming into focus. Maybe she *had* seen him before. His hands were sweaty, he desperately wanted another cigarette, but wasn't about to put down the phone.

"Alex says he might have something for you, that you should call him tomorrow, and," she added, with a hint of laughter, "that I should give him back his phone. I gotta go."

"Dusty Springfield," he said, in an effort to hold her. "Isn't that a little before your time?"

"No accounting for taste. I'll be at the store tomorrow. You should come by."

She hung up and DJ felt his heart buoyed.

In the morning, he'd have to take David by the house, and David being David, there was no telling how long they'd be and how much help he would end up needing beyond the ride. But maybe DJ could swing by the antiques store with Elise after school, save her from at least part of another afternoon spent holed up in her room.

Meaning to open the record player himself, DJ passed through the living room. David had propped his pillows on one end of the couch, and sat staring out the window, his legs extended across the cushions, his head turned toward the empty street. DJ bent down to grab the box from the floor, and before he straightened, he caught David swiping his eyes.

"Are you ... you're crying?"

"*I'm not*," David said, though he clearly had been. "Fucking Salinger." He reached between the cushions and the sofa-back, tossed the book across the floor.

"*Hey*," said DJ. It was an early paperback edition, its cover a garish painting of Holden in half-profile from behind, standing on a gritty street with a suitcase in his hand. The pages were yellowed, the glue of the spine disintegrating, and on impact a section had slid away and nearly split from the rest of the book. "That was mine."

DJ set the box on the dining table and picked up the book. He slid the loosened pages back into place and smoothed his hand across the cover. "Phoebe?"

"Yeah," David said, and held out his hand.

In the novel, Holden's little sister Phoebe is a year younger than Elise, but shares the same watchful concern and sharp wit, and Phoebe's vulnerability—her abiding love for the floundering Holden—would've given David pause. DJ gave him the book and glanced back at the box. "I was gonna set it up in her room, but maybe I should do it in here." Against the wall across from the couch, a maple sideboard stood on spindly legs, its surface clear but for a cone-shaped vase made of hand-blown glass. Robin's-egg blue, with a small circular base and a wide royal-blue rim. The turquoise of the record player and the Platter-Pak would fit right in.

"As long as it's light—she's got that thing packed with table linens and your grandparents' silver—or used to anyway."

"My grandparents' silver?"

"Somebody's silver in a velvet-lined case. Photo albums

and God knows what. You should see if Elise wants to help you."

At first, she said no, but then, as DJ was opening the box, she'd gone down to the basement to fetch Connie's 45s. He set the suitcase-like player down on the sideboard and let Elise undo the latch and remove all the bits of protective plastic. He scooped those back into the box, unwound the cord, and plugged it in. "Looks like it belongs here, right? What should we play?"

"You're the deejay," said David, and Elise turned to him in surprise.

"I thought those were his initials."

"They are. D for David, like me, and J for Jerome."

"Not Jerome," said DJ. "That's an old joke, between me and your mom—though I don't know why we thought it was so funny. The sound of it, I guess. Constance and *Jerome*," he drew out the "o" as if to say, *isn't that fancy now*. "It's actually Jasper—just as hoity-toity. I don't know why she liked Jerome."

"All right, Jasper Jerome," David said, "you gonna put on a record?"

"Yeah, yeah." He flicked through the case but couldn't make up his mind.

"*Lisey*," said David. "Help your old uncle out. Just pick one."

"Can I?"

DJ slid the case toward her, and she pulled out a black-labeled 45.

"'I'm into Something Good,'" she said. "Herman's Hermits—*really?* Should I pick something else?"

"No, it's good." DJ set the record on the turntable and brought down the needle. As soon as he heard the hand claps and strummed the guitar, he felt a giddy lift. The pleasure of that old song, its lyrics harking back to Andrea, and how she'd sung to him over the phone. Peter Noone singing about the new girl he's met in the neighborhood, bringing the verse around to the title's rhyme. Like the Salinger, this record had been DJ's, then passed down to Connie. He wouldn't—he couldn't—leave now. Not after David's mess; not after everything he'd promised. But Andrea... who knew? Maybe she'd be his way back to Brooklyn.

"Little corny," said Elise, her head bobbing to the beat. "But I like it."

"Sounds like the Beach Boys," said David.

"It's actually by Carole King—the music. Lyrics by Gerry Goffin, her writing partner and husband back then."

"Which means nothing to me, though you remain the king of trivia."

Only as DJ said the words, did he recall the other facts of the song—originally written for Earl Jean McCrea of The Cookies, who'd been pregnant with Goffin's baby, an infidelity he made brazenly public. You could learn too much from reading *Rolling Stone*.

Elise hummed along with the melody. "It's bubbly, but it's good."

"A music critic in the making," said David.

"*Da-ad*," she said, a classic diphthong of pleasure and embarrassment, as though the upbeat quality of the song made it too hard to maintain her aloof position.

"It *is* very Beach Boys," DJ said, at the song's surfy break, but David's chin was raised with a smile meant for someone else, and DJ turned toward the kitchen doorway and saw Connie. "Hey—you're home."

"I'm somewhere," she said. "1966?"

"'64," said DJ. "It's for you—the record player."

"It's cute, right?" said Elise.

"It is that."

"Aw, c'mon, Connie," said DJ. "Put something on."

"All right, all right." She set down her bag and began sifting through the records.

There was a feeling, a good feeling that had once been a daily part of DJ's life, the particular joy of putting on the perfect song—the one whoever you were playing it for had loved, missed, or somehow forgotten. All the tapes he'd made, all the CDs he'd burned, all the music he'd played in his Brooklyn living room. Songs that said to their listener: *I know you.*

"I can't choose," she said. "You pick one, honey."

"I don't know the songs," said Elise. "And I picked the last one."

"Okay—here's something." Connie held the record so they couldn't see, then turned to face them with a wait-for-it smile.

"*Toto?*" David and DJ said together at the first plinking notes.

"Why do you even have that?" said DJ.

"You gave it to me."

"I did?"

"As a joke, I hope," said David.

"When you worked at that record shop, near Bloomingdale's. You didn't see it when you had them spread all over my kitchen table?"

"I must've missed it somehow."

"Hate to break up this trip down memory lane, but I gotta get out of these clothes. You all figure out what to order for dinner." She picked up her bag, kissed Elise on the top of her head, and headed down the hall.

When the song ended, DJ didn't put on another. It had been a good moment—Elise playing that first record, David giving him the usual hard time—but his gift, like everything else in Hurley, didn't add up to what he'd hoped. In the end, his sense was that it had only made Connie sad—the last thing he wanted.

He looked back at the photos on her mantle, wondered who took the one with David and Elise. She'd drifted down the hall after Connie, David thumbed back through the Salinger to where he'd left off—maybe Holden on his way to find the ducks in Central Park, with the record for Phoebe still safely under his arm. DJ lifted the 45 from the turntable, tucked it back in with the rest, closed and latched the Platter-Pak, and then the player. Despite the havoc David managed to wreak these past few days, his departure would fall hard on them all.

8

Once again, DJ found himself in front of the antiques store—this time with Elise in tow, and the pleasing certainty of finding Andrea inside. But waiting for Elise in the pick-up line and even now, as he made a U-turn to grab the spot opening across the street, he found it hard to shake his morning's trip with David to the foreclosed house.

The place was surprisingly in order, the porch steps a patchwork of old and new wood. He still needed help getting in and out of the car, but insisted on managing the stairs himself, which was fine with DJ, bracing and lifting him an awkward strain for them both. What was plain, the wrecked truck aside, was that David had already been intent on leaving. Whether his getaway was due to his careless loss of the house or something more dire, DJ didn't ask, but a messenger bag and a canvas duffel were laid out on the bed, and all he had to do, at David's instruction, was grab a pair of running shoes from the closet and pull some clothes from the dresser drawers—a disconcerting reversal of his unpacking a few days before.

In the epitome of ironic moments, DJ found himself on the verge of asking David what he planned to do about the rest of his stuff—was he just gonna leave everything in the house? Then he remembered how Connie said it'd be months and months before the bank would evict him. If he'd asked, maybe they'd have had a good laugh. But David's mood was subdued, like someone stoically enduring the final phase of a punishment, and this seemed almost sadder than the rest. Like DJ, he'd brought it down upon himself, but it was more an expression of escalating failure and desperation. Where DJ let his world collapse, David made wild, if ill-conceived and coke-fueled, attempts to rebuild his. The fresh planks of wood, the cork flooring in Connie's basement—he'd still been trying to find a way to do right by her. When they got back to Connie's, David simply said thanks, then took up refuge on the couch. Would things have played out the same, would he still be leaving, if DJ weren't here?

The parking space was tighter than he'd realized, and once the lane was clear DJ pulled forward for a second try.

"Uncle D.?" said Elise, as a car came up behind him.

"Hang on," DJ turned and waved for them to move past.

"I don't think they're going anywhere."

"Oh, for crying out loud." He rolled his window down and yelled, *Go around.* Idiot, he might have added, if Elise weren't beside him. But the car, a beat-up black Camaro, only continued to idle behind them. "Seriously?" he said. "I can wait as long as the next guy."

"Is that a good idea?" said Elise.

DJ glanced back. "What's he gonna do? I was here first."

Elise nodded toward the driver's side. "That's not what he thinks."

The car was slowly pulling up beside them, close enough that, had he wanted to, DJ couldn't open his door. He couldn't pull forward either—not without risking damage to one or both cars. "Oh, for fuck's sake," he said, and then, "*Sorry.*" He felt an anxious flutter in his chest, could just picture what Connie would say.

The man in the Camaro filled the driver's seat, his face a slab with a bitter mouth drawn across it. "It's all right," he said to Elise, but he wasn't so sure.

As the passenger-side window of the Camaro rolled

down, the man leaned toward him. "You had your chance, and you didn't make it."

"*I had my chance?*" DJ knew better but couldn't help himself. "Are you kidding me?"

"Uncle D."

"With all due respect," DJ said, clearly having none, "I just needed a better angle. And let's not forget that I was here first."

The man in the Camaro cut his engine and got out of the car.

"Shit," said DJ, and rolled up his window. "Lock your door."

"You've done it now," said Elise. "Why are people so crazy about their cars?"

The man was fiendishly tall, a gray cashmere sweater only accentuating his crude bearing; the Hulk and Bruce Banner combined. Taking his sweet time, he came around, sat on the hood of the Camaro, and pushed up his sleeves. He grinned with chilling pleasure, then moved his mouth broadly as he said, "You're not gonna fit."

DJ held up his hands. "Okay, okay."

"*Say it,*" the man said, leaning close to the windshield. Elise reached for the door.

"No, no, no," said DJ, holding her arm. Then he said to the man, as loudly as he could through the glass, "I'm not gonna fit."

"Good boy," the man said, slapping the hood before he got back in his car.

The Camaro pulled back and DJ drove forward, took the first turn, and immediately pulled over at a hydrant. "Jesus Christ. I'm *so* sorry. Please don't tell your mom."

"That guy," said Elise, her eyes wide.

"Certifiable."

"And a dick."

DJ laughed. "*And a dick.*" A sliver of the Senate House

was visible at the end of the street. "You still up for the antiques store?"

"Yeah—I'm okay."

DJ's heart was only now slowing, a slight tremble still working his legs. *Fight or flight,* he thought with derision. *What about surrender?* "If it's all the same to you, I think we'll park a few blocks away."

"Wouldn't it be funny—"

"If he were buying antiques?" They both laughed, a bit of hysteria between them, that for DJ dissolved into a choking cough. Out of absurd ego and pure stupidity, he'd taken a terrible risk.

When they entered the store, Andrea was wrapping up a colonial-looking pitcher and washbasin, the buyer a man who kept saying, a little too loudly, how damn happy his wife was going to be. Probably nothing more than obnoxious, but having had enough of a scare for one day, DJ gave him a wide berth.

"*Hey—hello,*" said Andrea. "I'll be right with you."

A little business-like, but had he really expected there'd never be other customers? He and Elise poked about, and DJ spotted a series of animal-shaped teapots he didn't recall. A fish, a turtle, an elephant—all in that same celadon glaze as the anniversary teapot he'd given Belinda.

"Those are kinda cool," said Elise, when he picked up the one made to look like a fish.

The weight of it was appealing, its large, grooved tail almost like a moose antler, the scales of its belly cut deep into the clay. Two smaller fish decorated each side, and an even smaller one, bent into a joyous curve as though breaching the water, formed the handle of the lid. Lipless, as if cut with a knife, the mouth-like spout seemed to be saying, *ooh.* Despite its charm, this teapot lacked the glossy smoothness, the liquid curves of the bearded man and his companionable deer. It would've eased his nerves to buy it, but he set it back down beside its fellow oddities.

"I like those, too," said Andrea, coming over to them now. "Not the fish so much, but the group of them together is sweet. What happened to your fine hat?" she asked Elise, making DJ realize he hadn't noticed its absence.

"School day," said Elise.

"Duh." Andrea tapped the base of her palm to her forehead.

"That's okay," said Elise, and DJ was touched by her easy pardon.

"*So*," said Andrea, turning her attention to him. "Did you bring me anything? No Dusty?"

"Oh—no. I mean, yes—I have it. It's just..." DJ scrambled for what to say. "My records—they're a little inaccessible right now."

"A little?" said Elise.

"What—why?" said Andrea, looking amused.

"When I moved," he began, but was reluctant to go into detail. "I couldn't be there when the movers delivered my stuff to a storage unit out on 28. Bit of a catastrophe."

"Oh, no—things got broken?"

"Hard to say. But probably. They just crammed everything in." The man's words echoed in his head. *You're not gonna fit.*

"Well, that's not very good." She glanced back toward the counter. "I have a number for you, but if you can't get to the records... How bad is it?"

Elise cleared her throat.

"I'm sorry," he said "What?"

"How bad is it?"

DJ gathered himself. "It's less than ideal, but my sister will help over the weekend. I was just waiting—"

"To hear from Alex. All right, all right," she said, half to herself, then to him, "because I vouched for you."

"Everything was well packed," he said, though it was only an assumption. Tracy, being who she was, would've taken care with the records, except he recalled a row of milk crates, safe for transport unless something were to be stacked on top.

"This weekend?" said Andrea.

"Starting Friday. While you're in school," he added when Elise looked his way.

"I could miss a day," she said.

"Yeah, I'm sure your mom would love that."

"Alex wants to come in on Saturday. Maybe I can help for a couple of hours."

Before he could think, he said, "Why would you do that?"

Andrea laughed. "I don't know. Sounds like you could use some help, and Alex will be pissed if you flake out. You're not going to flake out, are you?"

"*No*," he said. "I am not."

"Good, then. Gives me something to do—I have no life up here. Thank God I'm going back to the city next week."

"Lucky you," he said, then smiled the best that he could.

Andrea gave him a store card with a handwritten number on the back. "Maybe don't call until you see what's what? He's very precious about his connections."

The door creaked open and two well-groomed men, DJ guessed a couple, came in. Andrea turned to them and smiled. "Let me know if I can help you with anything."

DJ looked at Elise, who tilted her head toward the door and whispered, "We should go."

"Sorry," said Andrea. She pulled a phone from her back pocket and opened her contacts. "Put your number in and I'll let you know about Saturday." The store phone rang and she held up her hands. "Wednesday afternoon. Who knew?"

DJ entered his number, decided against putting

123

something funny in the notes, and set her phone on the end of the counter. He tried to catch her eye, but she'd already pulled out Alex's appointment book and was flipping through the pages, saying she was sure something could be arranged. Only as they left did he realize he'd failed to ask after her newborn niece.

Outside, the Camaro was gone, the space sitting open.

"Look at that," said Elise.

"Figures," he said, and then, as they began walking to the car. "Think I have a shot?"

"Hard to say. She likes you. But she didn't give you her number."

"Yeah, I noticed that, too—though she did say she would call. And her brother's taking a cut."

Elise shrugged, as if to say, *we'll see*. "How many records do you have?"

He tried to calculate, ticking off the shelves of his old record room. "Twelve hundred?" he said, then remembered the crates. "Maybe fifteen?"

"Wow. That's a lot. You could have your own store."

"Practically. Can I never interest you in getting soft serve?"

"Okay, okay. But only because you look like you need it."

"What about you, Miss Unruffled? I'm really sorry about before."

"It's fine—I'm fine."

"Are you?" he said. "Because this can't be easy, with me here, and your Dad—"

Elise made her buzzer sound. "I don't want to talk about that."

"I'm just saying you can, if you want to."

"Well, I don't. And I don't need *ice cream*—I'm not a child."

"That makes one of us. Still want to go to Rhino?"

"I have homework," she said, walking ahead.

Of course she did, but she could hardly be eager to get to it. What she wanted was to be by herself, and he could hardly blame her. How many ways had he overstepped? "Sorry I dragged you," he said, catching up. "And then that guy—"

"Can you stop? You didn't. *I'm fine*," she added, refuting the tears that were choking her words.

"Let's both stop. Just for a second. Please."

Elise stopped, but she wouldn't look at him. DJ reached into his pockets for a tissue, a handkerchief, but all he had were his cigarettes. "We'll just go home, okay? Please don't cry."

"Because that's your territory?"

"King of tears. But you win this round."

They walked the rest of the way without speaking, but side by side.

As they got in the car she said, "Did you know that he built us a tree house?"

"At Connie's?" he said, confused.

"At the old house—for me and Jenn. *Her* father is a creep. Mine is just…"

DJ wasn't about to fill in that blank. "Jenn's your friend who moved away?"

Elise closed her eyes and exhaled, then buckled her seatbelt and pushed on. "It had a hook on a higher branch, so you could pull up the ladder. And a bench with a secret compartment. My dad has a thingy—a drum… a Dremel—that he helped us use to carve our names on a little sign. He's not a bad person," she added, her voice strangling again.

"No one said he was."

"Then why is he going away?" she said, fully crying now.

"Sometimes people…" he started, searching for a tack, but she looked at him sharply and he said, "I don't know."

DJ opened the glove box, where there were tissues

galore, all in tidy little packets. He did not look forward to Connie asking about their day.

Meaning to sleep in, DJ set no alarm. If asked, he might say he was giving Connie and David space—it'd be hard enough after they met with their lawyer. However coincidental, it was as if his arrival had created combustion, like he'd tripped a wire or set match to the fuse running from separation to divorce. He didn't need to witness the last moments of what was left of their marriage.

It was almost comical to think back on his fantasy of leaving Belinda—that was all it seemed to him now. *Leaving*. It sounded a simple enough thing. Though he wouldn't have gone far, just moved from Park Slope to Sarah's much smaller Manhattan apartment. With little of value to divide, and no kid between them, it had still been a deal-breaking imperative that he keep Belinda in his life, which, in hindsight, had guaranteed it never getting that far. The very idea of them sitting before a lawyer, signing their names by little sticky-note arrows—he'd never have been able to do it. He would've folded before they left the apartment, wouldn't have been able to bring himself to even schedule the appointment. The difference here, he supposed, that it became inevitable. A severing they both wanted, if to varying degrees; being together more impossible than being apart. Then, of course, there was the question of Elise—what was best for her. Amidst anger and frustration, worry, fear and disappointment, Connie's resolve was unwavering. She wanted David to remain a part of their daughter's life. What went on in David's mind, it was harder to say. It seemed as though he'd given up, resigned himself to letting Elise slip further and further away, Holden Caulfield with pieces of broken record in his pocket.

DJ shifted his pillow and rolled onto his back, the cushions sliding slightly beneath him. Unless he heard from her otherwise, Connie would pick up Elise, either with or without David. *Depending on the time,* she'd said, though what it likely depended on was how it went. He wished he'd could've gone to the antiques store today, when he had nothing to do, wished he wasn't waiting on her call. *A little flighty,* Alex had said. Would she really come to Catskill Park Storage? Did he really want her to? He had to dig out his records, regardless, organize for potential sale, figure out what he was going to do with the rest of his stuff. He was waiting to hear from Tracy, too. Waiting, waiting. Hens to roost, all his shoes and axes to fall. And then what? He'd be damned if he knew. Then he'd have to gather them all up again. He hadn't wanted to start over; he'd just wanted to go on. Head tucked down into the sleeping bag, he blindly felt his way along the coffee table for his phone and made sure the ringer was on.

DJ dozed till he heard footsteps above.

"*Hey,*" he called.

"It's just me," Connie called back.

Disconcerted, he made his way up the stairs.

"I'm making fresh," she said, pulling coffee grounds from the freezer. "All slept out?"

"I was just coming up for a shower."

The look she gave him was skeptical.

"So maybe not just. Where's David?"

"I dropped him at the mall. Said he wanted to get a haircut, pick up a few things before he goes. I'll scoop him up after I get Elise. I didn't feel like waiting."

"And that sounded plausible to you?"

"You know what?" She laid a filter into the basket of the coffee maker, added spoonfuls of coffee with a sharp flick of her wrist. "If he wants to do one more stupid thing before he goes, I'm hardly in a position to stop him. I'm not his keeper. I'm not even his wife anymore. Or I won't be once the papers are filed with the court."

"I think that's enough coffee," said DJ.

"What? Aw, shit." She spooned some of the grounds back into the bag. "To tell you the truth, I think he wants to get her a present. Though I don't know what he thinks he's gonna find at the mall that'll make up for his taking off."

He and Elise had found the porkpie hat, but he kept that thought to himself. "So the lawyer—it went okay?"

"Heartbreakingly easy."

"*Oh, Conners*," he said, but she waved him off.

"Go take your shower, Deej. I'm fine."

"Not convincing," he said, walking down the hall without looking back.

"I know. But I will be. I don't have a choice."

Your life was one thing, then one day you signed a paper, you got on a bus, and it was something else.

David's departure was marked by one of those sparkling spring days, the morning cool but brightly sunny, with the promise of warming. Just as they were leaving the house—DJ set to take him to the bus; Connie set to drop Elise at school then meet up at the storage unit—Connie changed her mind. Stopping DJ in the carport, she said under her breath, "What if it's the last time?" Freed from his marriage, his life, whatever debts he might owe or be due from his so-called friends, David's return to Hurley seemed less and less likely.

They'd made their real goodbyes the night before, sitting around the living room. David in his usual spot on the couch, DJ on the other end, Connie sunk into the armchair with Elise perched on its arm, the minutes ticking all-too consciously by.

Of David's fresh haircut, Connie said, "Women only

cut their hair when they mean to change something more than their appearance."

But men cut their hair all the time, he and David contended, as did any woman who wore her hair short.

"I hate getting haircuts," Elise threw in, not protesting when Connie pulled her onto her lap. "All that hoopla," she went on. "The squeak and bump as they adjust your seat. All that spritzing and gossipy chatter."

"And those slippery capes," DJ added with an exaggerated shudder.

"*Yes,*" said Elise, slapping her hand down on the arm of the chair. Then she'd rolled her head back to look at Connie. "*See?* They're so icky."

DJ had been grateful for the jovial moment, but it didn't last.

"You know what makes me sad?" David said. "That fucking tree house."

"David," said Connie.

"Sorry. I just hate the idea of somebody else's kids playing in there."

DJ looked at Elise, but she wouldn't meet his eye.

"I'm too old for that, anyway," she'd said, slipping off Connie's lap.

Now here they were, reassembled at the Greyhound station, the air full of diesel fumes, David looking back one last time from the steps of the bus. He'd given them all gift cards to Barnes & Noble, his trite choice mitigated by the personal notes he'd carefully penned on each little envelope. *For what it's worth,* DJ's said, *I'm glad we went fishing.*

After the bus had passed from view, Connie took Elise in the borrowed Focus and DJ followed in her Civic, the radio loud, the college station playing, of all the songs in the world, Iggy Pop's "Lust for Life," as they headed for Home

Depot. "You're not going to want to lay things out on the dirt," she'd said, and DJ, despite struggling to imagine how it was all going to work, had obligingly replied, "Good idea."

Elise steered their cart down the long aisles, DJ trailing behind as Connie added supplies. Two large blue plastic tarps, a box of contractor demolition bags, a roll of packing tape—in case he wanted to open and then seal something back up—and a six-pack of water. At the register, there was a display of baseball hats and she tossed three of them in, along with three Snickers bars, then sent Elise in search of a bottle of sunscreen.

"We should pick up sandwiches, too," she said, and DJ understood that today of all days Connie needed a project.

"Okay," he said, but it didn't satisfy her.

"Once we start pulling stuff out, we're not going to be able to just leave it."

"Yeah, yeah—that makes sense."

From the end cap, she picked out a flashlight and a pack of D batteries and tossed those in, too. "DJ," she said. "What am I doing here?"

"Next guest," said the cashier.

DJ pushed the cart forward. "It's all right—it's gonna be all right."

"Found it," said Elise, breathlessly coming up behind them. She waggled the orange tube. "They only had 30 SPF, though."

Connie rubbed her face with both hands, held them to her mouth, then released them to reveal a newly fortified smile. "That'll have to do."

DJ began passing items to the cashier.

"Did I miss something?" said Elise.

"Your mom was just saying we should get some sandwiches."

"A little storage-park picnic," said Connie, "for when we take a break."

"We'll definitely need that." Elise rested her chin on the handle of the cart. "You think he's coming back?"

"I don't know," said Connie. "I hope so."

"One eleven seventy-six," said the cashier.

DJ rummaged through the bags. "That's too much. Can we put one of these tarps back? And how much for the demo bags?"

"You're gonna need those if stuff is broken," Connie said, coming up close behind him, and DJ felt his whole body sag.

The cashier held up the tarp he'd put aside. "You gonna take this, or no?"

"Taking," said Connie, reaching into her purse.

"Don't do that," he said, but she handed the cashier her card.

"We can always return one, if we don't use it."

"That's hardly the point."

"Well," she said, lightly tapping her fist on his back. "We can fight about it later, okay?"

"Can we just go?" said Elise.

"Yes, sweetie, we're going."

Elise hefted the plastic bags from the cart. "*Sweetie*," she said to DJ. "That's never a good sign."

At the storage unit, DJ rolled up the door, things no better or worse, just the same jammed-up tangle he recalled. "Can we picnic first?"

"You wish," said Connie. "What's your plan?"

"My plan?" They'd all sunscreened their faces and arms at her behest, donned their caps like a diminutive team, but he had no plan—he'd assumed that she would. "Find the record boxes? There's milk crates, too—bring that all up to the front so that I can show them?"

"You found a buyer?"

"Possibly."

"So you think we can pull stuff out, then put it back with the records in front."

"Not really."

Connie adjusted the brim of her hat. "How many boxes are we talking about?"

"Twenty? Maybe more? Half a dozen milk crates?"

"*Careful,*" she said to Elise, who'd started tugging at one of the black garbage bags.

"It's packed in pretty solid," Elise said.

She and Connie spread out one of the tarps while DJ, reminded of Sarah in his Brooklyn apartment, borrowed a folding chair from the office.

"I'll stand and pull," said Connie. "Deej—you be ready to take the weight."

In this fashion they removed the top layer of bulging bags, some filled with clothes, according to Tracy's careful hand, others with decorative pillows and bedding. DJ set the mini amp aside. He could sell that too, along with the cords and pedals, if they came across them, since there'd be no more electric guitars. He tried to think of these things as not having belonged to him, a pile of stuff at someone else's stoop sale, all easily sold for a few bucks, but the pit of his stomach told him otherwise. It was the stupid hats, more than anything—the tender goofiness of Connie's gesture, the way she'd tossed them into the cart—that made him feel like he had to go through with it now, even if he also felt like he might throw up.

Below the bags were various-sized boxes, labeled by room, and they began laying them out that way.

"We should spread out that second tarp," Connie said. "You might as well organize as long as we're doing it."

"What's 'middle room'?" asked Elise.

"Those'll be heavy—mostly books."

"Ooh—can we open one?"

"Not now," said Connie.

"*Fine,*" said Elise. "How about a Snickers then?"

"Be my guest, but bring me a water."

"There's probably a lot of books she'd like," DJ said, the realization cheering him.

"I'm sure," said Connie, "and that's nice. But if we start opening stuff now …"

"Records, records. I got it."

By the time they broke for lunch it looked like a yard sale, just from the bits of furniture they'd hauled out—the Formica table and vinyl-seated chairs, the metal-shaded lamp, a taboret cart Belinda had used to store art supplies—and a couple of passing cars had slowed. The array of boxes had begun to look like a floorplan for his old apartment, but they'd yet to find a single one labeled records.

"It's like they *knew,*" Connie said.

Still, the day was lovely and warm and as they wiped their brows and opened their sandwiches, a good feeling hung between them—more than you would expect, considering how the day had begun.

"You've got a lot of stuff," said Elise, her mouth full of egg salad, which had made them all laugh so hard, he'd had to slap Connie on the back to keep her from choking.

After they'd settled down, Connie said, "I think you have to rent another smaller unit—just for a month. If you put everything you're gonna sell in there, it'll be much easier to get the rest of it back in here, until you decide what you're gonna do with it. Otherwise, I don't know. It's already one o'clock." She took off her hat and smoothed back her hair. "What do you say?"

With what she'd already spent and Alex taking his cut, it would barely be worth selling the records, but he didn't want to go on paying to keep them either. "Okay," he said.

Connie clapped her hands. "All right then. Off you go."

When DJ returned, dangling the key to a smaller unit on the building's short side, Connie frowned, as if in painful apology, and tilted the top of the carton she held in her arms toward him.

MIXED ROOMS it read, followed by a hyphen and the words BELINDA ART. There'd been bags of her clothes, and the one with her comforter, but he couldn't pretend what was in this box was from someone else's stoop sale.

Connie said, "I couldn't just put it on a random pile. You should take it home."

He held the box to his chest but seemed unable to move.

Elise touched his arm. "You want me to put it in the car?"

"Okay," he said, "Yeah."

"It's light. Is it like drawings and stuff?"

"Might be. But she made these boxes... they're hard to describe."

"It's a box of boxes?"

A light laugh escaped him, and it was as if he'd been trapped underwater then suddenly dragged to the surface, fresh air refilling his lungs. "Something like that. I can show you later."

"You're good with her," Connie said, as Elise crunched along the gravel to the car. "She doesn't take to people easily."

"Well, neither do I."

"Oh, stop. You're like the most people-est person I know."

"The most *people-est*?"

Connie laughed now, too, a small chuckling sound that was like further resuscitation, but then her smile faded, and he turned to follow her gaze. "Case in point."

A red VW Rabbit had pulled in from the road, Elise raised her hand to the woman getting out. *Andrea*.

"I don't suppose she's coming to help," said Connie.

"She said she might, but not till tomorrow. And she said she'd call."

"Well, don't just stand there—go on."

"I would've told you," he said, "if I'd known."

"It's fine."

"Don't say *that*."

"Go," she said. "Go."

But Andrea and Elise were already walking toward them, so all he wound up doing was taking a slight step forward. "How'd you find us?"

"Nice to see you again," she said, bending past him toward Connie.

"Likewise," said Connie, and DJ made a half-turn so they formed a small circle.

"There's only one other storage place on 28," Andrea said. "I know I said I could help tomorrow, but Molly's not doing so great. My sister-in-law—she's just had a baby," she added for Connie's benefit, and DJ had to wonder if the beaming attention she'd shown him was just who she was, that sort of person. *Chandeliers.* Twinkling light. "Anyway, my brother—he doesn't want to leave her alone."

"Oh," said Connie. "I'm sorry to hear that."

Andrea craned her head to peek into the unit, which was still crammed half-full, then turned to take in the growing city of stuff they'd laid out on the tarps. "Looks like you're making some headway." She'd had to close the store, she explained, to deliver some Queen Anne chairs to a valued customer, up in Woodstock. "It's actually shorter to go this way, and you guys were hard to miss. A very hat-y family."

"She didn't want us to die of sunstroke," said Elise.

"Not *die*," said Connie. "But, you know."

The look she exchanged with Andrea was the kind of mild reproach women often share, as if to say, *Without us, then what?* A look that compounded DJ's disappointment, turning it in on himself. For all Connie's caring for everyone else, who in the world was looking out for her? She'd taken him in, included him in her life in every possible way, and even under the auspices of helping her out, all he'd done was add to her responsibilities.

"I should get going," Andrea said, then looked to DJ. "Feels like I'm always saying that, right?"

"Don't want to keep people waiting for their Queen Annes."

"*No,*" she said, her sardonic laugh only making her more appealing. "I was supposed to go home next week. Now I don't know. So maybe I'll see you."

"Where's home?" Connie asked.

"Brooklyn—Park Slope."

"*That's* funny," said Elise.

"Why's that?"

"He just moved from there."

"From Park Slope? Why didn't you say?"

"Didn't get a chance."

"So, I have seen you before."

"Probably."

"Teeny tiny world," Andrea said. "Well, I really am going now."

"C'mon, Lisey," said Connie. "Back to work."

"Thanks for coming by," said DJ.

"Sorry I couldn't help."

"Sorry about your sister-in-law."

"Let me know what happens with Alex's guy," she called back on her way to the car. "And don't forget my Dusty."

"You sure you got records in there?" Connie said, stacking another box on the tarp. She thumped his shoulder as she passed him again. "Chop, chop, *mon frère*. She definitely likes you, but there's something else. *Someone* else, I'd say, if I had to put money on it."

DJ thought of the O'Jays' plunking bass, the word *money* sung in echoing refrain. He followed Connie into the unit, where the chifforobe rose like a monument. How long would he hang on to that ridiculous piece of furniture?

It happened too quickly for him to understand what he was seeing at first. Elise heaving a carton, the bundle of a black garbage bag tumbling forward, her small sneaker in front of the foot of the chifforobe, its bulky weight almost dancing as it tipped. Connie saying, *whoa, whoa, whoa,* as she tried to brace it. A drawer slipped free, then the whole damn thing flopped forward and smashed to the ground, clipping Elise's arm as it knocked her to the side. Then he and Connie were both scrambling over and around the snapped pieces of white-painted wood, dust and the smell of cigarette ash filling his nostrils, Elise softly crying, *my arm, my arm.*

"Get her legs," Connie said. "Elise, honey, I'm going to lift from under your shoulders, try to keep your body stiff, okay?"

Every TV show, every movie he'd ever seen—someone taped to a board, someone screaming not to move them. But they'd already carried her from the shadowed storage space into the glaring afternoon light, set her gently down on one of the retro chairs, still spread out in their lunch-time formation.

"I'm all right," said Elise, left arm clasped across her chest, right hand cupping her elbow. "That thing really whacked me, though." She slowly straightened, then re-bent her arm. "I couldn't do that if it was broken, right?"

"We're gonna get you an X-ray right now and find out. Help me get her to the car."

"I can walk."

"I'm just going to take your other arm then, all right?" To him, Connie said, "You've got a couple of hours of daylight left. Maybe Andrea can come back and help you. Maybe she knows someone."

"Maybe she knows someone?"

"I don't know, Deej—you're gonna have to figure it out. You got extra space now—just drag it all back in and I'll call you from the hospital."

The first thing DJ did after they left was sit down and light a cigarette. But he couldn't settle. Cigarette dangling from his lips, he tore the packaging off the flashlight Connie had bought and put in the batteries. Then he went into the unit, clambered over the broken pieces of the chifforobe and up onto the box Elise had been trying to move, and swept the beam across the back half of the space.

Son of a bitch, he said and flicked ash into the open area behind him. Where the Rube Goldberg of a heavy trash bag full of towels and sheets had freed itself from the chaos behind the chifforobe, the light caught the round knobs of his bedroom dresser, and stacked on top of that, three milk crates of records. He stubbed his cigarette out against the wall, reached for one of the crates. He could touch it but was too far away to grasp or lift it up.

He kicked and dragged the pieces of the chifforobe over to one side. Shoved cartons and hauled bags, pushed an already dented file cabinet toward the front, metal shrieking against the concrete floor. Once he'd cleared a wide enough opening to squeeze through, he hoisted one of the crates up and onto his shoulder, carried it out and set it down on the gravel. Then he Googled Alex's store and left Andrea a message. *Elise may have broken her arm, Connie took her to the ER, and I'm here with my goddamn records trying to put everything away again before it gets dark. If there's any way you can see to helping me, I'd be forever in your debt. This is DJ,* he added, *in case you couldn't guess.*

It felt great, for once, to give voice to his desperation. It wasn't like he'd had much of a shot with her anyway, and he had no one else to call. He unwrapped a Snickers, downed half a bottle of water, and went back to work, stopped only by the ring of his phone.

"It's Andrea. What happened?"

"She got knocked over by a chifforobe."

"A chifforobe?"

138

"It's like a wardrobe, but with—"

"I know what a chifforobe is. I just can't believe that you *have* one."

"*Had,*" he said, surveying the wreckage. It was a good thing Connie insisted he get those contractor bags.

"I'm still in Woodstock—I just called into the store. I could stop on my way back. Maybe half an hour?"

"That'd be fantastic."

"I mean I could maybe give you half an hour."

"Beats nothing," he said.

"I'm so sorry—I hope she's all right."

"Yeah—me, too."

Having excavated another pair of milk crates, DJ could now partially see the trove of record cartons, stacked against the back wall. He hauled out the remains of the chifforobe, then began pushing and dragging stuff over to either side. He'd just been shoving the last of the end tables and some bigger boxes that blocked his access when he heard a car ease onto the gravel. He wove his way back outside, sweaty and disheveled, but ecstatic to see her.

"Any word?" Andrea called, walking up to meet him.

He shook his head.

She crouched down to examine the crates. "Not exactly mint."

He looked back into the unit. "It's gonna be more about quantity, I'm afraid."

"There's more?"

"Oh, yeah. There's a bunch of cartons. I'm only now digging them out. Then all of *that,*" he said, with a dismissive sweep of his arm toward the tarps, "has to come back in."

"So you said. I might have just the thing to help you."

"I hope it's Advil."

From the hatchback of her car, Andrea pulled out a hand truck, steered it bumpily toward him.

"Ta da!" she said, spinning it around to a stop.

What a stupidly simple thing—all the needless lifting and dragging they'd done. Without thinking, DJ stepped forward, took her face in his hands, and kissed her full on the lips.

"Well, okay," she said.

"Sorry," he said, moving back. "It's just been . . ."

"Such a day?"

"*Such* a day. You want a water? I've got Snickers." If he just kept spilling out words maybe his kiss could be overrun, disregarded, if that's what she wanted. "I can't thank you enough."

"It's all right. What's your plan?"

DJ wished people would quit asking him that, but this time he had one. The hand truck made quick work of moving the crates and cartons of records into the smaller unit. Then all the boxes labeled Living and Middle Room that seemed likely, by their weight, to hold books. There were four large plastic bins full of Kodak film boxes and other archival files, and they wheeled those in, too, DJ doing his best to ignore that pernicious number. Then Andrea had to go.

"You're a photographer?" she asked as he slid the last bin off the hand truck.

"My wife."

"Oh," she said, unable to hide her surprise.

"She died. Three years ago, come May."

"Oh, God—all this stuff. I'm so sorry."

"Yeah."

"You can keep the hand truck over the weekend. I doubt Alex will need it."

"That'd be great—thanks so much for helping."

"I didn't do much."

"But you did."

"Well . . ." she said, with a wincing smile of regret. "I really should get going."

He laughed, thanked her again, and walked her to her car. "Don't see many of these anymore."

"Hand-me-down from Alex. Mostly so I can haul his shit around."

"I hear that." DJ's gaze skipped from the gravel at his feet to the boxes on the tarps, over the red roof of her car toward the road—anywhere but directly at her. He was stalling, but was she? When he did look her way, the frames of her glasses caught the light, that same flash of metallic blue as the first time he'd seen her. Weren't some things meant to be?

They each moved forward, a shimmy this way and that, a shared laugh as they bumped into a hug, their arms clasping awkwardly, then more firmly to each other. He bent his head slightly to rest his forehead against hers, but it was Andrea who turned her face up for the kiss. Softer, quieter, a kind of question: are we doing this? Then she pulled back, her face still close to his.

"I can't—this is so—"

"I know," he said. "Everything's—"

"*Right?*" she said, with more enthusiasm than he would've liked. "Alex'll be pissed if he knows how long— and that's just…" She dropped her arms and DJ let his fall away.

"You need to go."

"I really do."

He stepped back so she could get in her car. "I'll call you," she said, holding her hand by her ear the way people still do though phones are nothing like they used to be. He held up his thumb, the corniest of gestures. Someone else, for sure—the pull between them strong, regardless.

While everything was torn apart—the kiss spiking his energy, running like a loop in his head—DJ rummaged around, turning over boxes and bags, bending this way and that to read labels, and setting aside a light oblong box labeled UKE and another labeled LIVING ROOM—DECORATIVE/

TCHOTCHKE. He'd dragged the pieces of the chifforobe out onto the gravel, then begun the thankless task of putting everything they'd pulled out back in, keeping what order he could, while racing what was left of the day. The hand truck made everything easier, but he could not remember the last time he'd worked this hard.

Finally, Connie called, and as DJ made his way outside for better reception, the ukulele box snagged his attention. On the back, Tracy had drawn a staff with a measure of notes whose melody he'd yet to decipher; something he meant to do before she called about his guitars. If Elise's arm was broken, it'd be a while before she could hold, let alone learn to play one. But Connie assured him that Elise's bones were intact, only her elbow badly sprained.

"Oh, thank God," he said, his body sliding down the wall of the storage unit until he was seated on a ragged edge of grass, the light beginning to slip into dusk. His arms and thighs ached, even his hands were sore from wielding the hand truck, whatever strength he'd had left seeping away in the wash of relief. "Can I talk to her?"

"She's a little out of it. We'll come there."

"Don't," he said, "I can finish it. Andrea lent me a hand truck."

"What about your cabinet thing? You'll need help with that."

"I've already dragged out the pieces."

"Well, you can't just *leave* them there."

"*Connie.*"

"What?"

"Come by if you want to, okay?"

After a moment she said, "So she helped you."

"For a little while—yeah."

"All right, then. We'll see you in a bit."

He didn't reassemble any of it, but he put the heavy Metro and lighter aluminum shelving in the smaller unit and locked it. One of the tarps was completely cleared, but he'd wait for Connie to fold it. He lay the larger sidepieces of the chifforobe across the back seat of her Civic, snapped apart what he could, and filled three contractor bags with the smaller sections. He thought about keeping the curved crown, but then stuffed it right in with the rest. He fit one bag in the trunk and settled the other two in the wells of the back seat, where they rose like ungainly passengers, and left the folding chair outside the closed office.

All afternoon he'd had his jacket off, but now he put it back on, sat down on one of the vinyl-seated chairs, put his feet up on another, and smoked the last cigarette in his pack. He was still sitting there watching the occasional car go by when Connie pulled in. There were just a few boxes and the dozen or so hulking bags left to go, his taking a break about the only thing he didn't feel guilty for.

She got out of the car, set a white paper bag on the hood, and DJ rose to meet her. They hugged, a long clasp of exhaustion and attenuated catastrophe. Elise rolled down her window, held out a tall white cup with a straw, as though making a toast.

"*Soft serve,*" she called, and he looked at Connie.

"We stopped for shakes. I got you chocolate."

DJ walked around to the passenger side. "How you doing, little E.?"

She looked down at the blue triangle of fabric supporting her arm. "I'm slung."

"I'm so sorry you got hurt."

"I know," she said, then closed the window and reclined her seat.

"Okay, then," he said, and walked back to Connie. "You sure you don't want to take her home?"

"Six of one. At least she's not thinking about him leaving. Or maybe she is. I can't get her to talk about it, so who the fuck knows."

David. How could he have forgotten the day's start?

"She wouldn't eat anything," Connie went on "and I didn't want her to have all that Motrin sitting on an empty stomach."

He drank half his shake, partly soupy but still good, and then, with Elise dozing in the car, the last of the color draining from the sky, he and Connie fit the rest of his stuff in the larger unit and folded the tarps.

DJ dangled the key. "You should just roll it down with me in there."

"It wasn't your fault," she said, and then, circling her hand as though wiping a mirror, "Well, all of this is—that you brought every stick of furniture up here, every bit and bob you've ever owned. But you don't need me to keep telling you that, do you?" She brought her hands to her face, then let them drop. "Is that what I do?"

"*No*," he said, but she looked at him. "Okay—yes."

"Anyway. I just wanted her with us, so if it's anyone's fault it's mine. Who knew some freaking bag of towels was gonna cause an avalanche?"

"Thank you," he said. "For helping—for everything."

"You're my brother."

"I am that," he said, then heaved down the rattling door.

9

DJ returned to Catskill Park Storage determined to conquer. He'd called the dealer Alex had referred him to and scheduled an appointment for Monday morning. He wouldn't bother cataloging, but he would open the cartons, arrange them in a way that made sense, and flip through for any albums with collectible value. Plus, he wanted to find the Dusty Springfield for Andrea, and anything else he might keep for sentiment's sake. Nothing classical, nothing novelty, but a top ten or twenty formative records—as though he'd be able to decide. *Don't get lost in there,* Connie had said as he was leaving, and then handed him a grocery list.

He moved the milk crates against one wall toward the front, then made a pair of central rows, each five cartons long and two wide, for easy access. He sliced through the tape and opened the flaps of each box, a realization slowly overtaking him.

While the crates held the records they'd held before, mostly classical and re-released compilation sets, the rest had simply been packed up as a person—or more likely people—pulled them off the shelves. A handful, even a chunk of albums, might reflect a section of his former idiosyncratic arrangement, which had been genre-ish, but more closely tied to favored artists and associative links, and had depended in part on muscle memory—the feeling of where a record would be. There'd been times when he couldn't lay his hands

145

on something he wanted, but the entire collection was now fully randomized. Each box packed tight, with just a thin layer of bubble-wrap laid across the top. There was no way he would find the record Andrea wanted or make an optimal display—not without spending the days he would need to deal with the larger unit.

His lifetime's collection of records was just an odd lot with a few potential treasures for someone else to find. DJ sat down on the cold cement floor and cried. He could download any song, buy any album he missed again, but that didn't make him or his records feel less obsolete. Like a disconnected lyric, the words *fire sale* drifted into his head. He would ask for five, hope for four hundred dollars, but come Monday morning, he knew he'd take whatever cash he could get.

For days, DJ had imagined swinging by the antiques store, the creak of the door as he walked in, the smile that would spread across Andrea's face as he lay the Dusty Springfield album on the counter before her. Instead, he Googled Goodwill, found there was a donation center at the mall. He locked the smaller unit and opened the larger one. Connie had suggested a tag sale, but he wasn't doing that. No amount of signage would bring more than a few people out here, and even if it did, he wasn't gonna sit around and watch strangers paw through and judge his things, half of which he and Belinda bought at yard and stoop sales themselves. An undoing he couldn't endure.

There was probably a dress, a blouse, an embroidered handkerchief of Belinda's he'd want to keep, but it was the same as the records. He couldn't bear going through them—then or now. So, he pulled out the bags accordingly labeled and loaded them into the car, one sitting in the passenger seat beside him as he drove. *Well, look at me*, he said, to Tracy and Connie, as much as himself. The highway stretched open before him, woods on either side, and DJ tried not to think of David escaping down to Silver Spring, not to feel like they'd traded places.

The young woman at the Goodwill was kind and warm for no particular reason, and DJ wanted to bow down and kiss her feet, but merely arranged for a pick-up late Sunday afternoon, took his yellow receipt, and said thanks. Then he drove to the Hannaford for the items on Connie's list.

When he got back to the house, Connie had reclaimed David's spot on the couch, Elise settled in the armchair, both of them reading.

"Something came for you from FedEx," said Connie, motioning toward the front hall.

"From FedEx?"

"Bigger than a bread box," she said, crisply turning the page of a hardcover book without a dust jacket.

DJ frowned, in no mood to take her guff, then he saw the package and his heart did a little flip. *The Yamaha.* "That's actually for Elise. Let me put the food away and we'll open it up."

"What is it?" said Elise.

"You'll see."

"Are you all right?" Connie asked.

"Not really," he said, moving into the kitchen. "I'm making coffee," he called back. "You want?"

"What'd I do?"

"Nothing," he said. "It's all me."

"Then yes, please."

"Trying to read here," said Elise, and he couldn't help but smile. It was a terrible drag that she'd have to wait to play it, but it was still a good gift.

"All right, all right," Connie said, once he'd brought in their coffee. "What's in the box?"

"Corrugated cardboard is us," said DJ, laying the box on the floor and once again cutting through packing tape. He looked up at Elise, who'd set down her book and leaned forward, minding her arm.

"I'm sorry you can't open it yourself, but I hope you like it."

"Just open it, will you?" said Connie.

"*Mom.*"

Tracy had packed the Yamaha in a hard case he hadn't owned. One more kindness was going to break him apart, but he went on unlatching the case and then lifted it out. "Here ya go."

"You got me a guitar?"

"Not quite—I had it. I'm selling the rest," he said, glancing at Connie, "but I'm giving this one to you."

"I can't even play." Elise started to cry.

"You will, honey," said Connie. "Just a couple of weeks."

"I know that." Elise struggled a little to stand, having only the one good arm to press herself up from the sunken cushion. "It's too much," she said to DJ. "You do too much. And I don't know *how*—does nobody see that? I don't know how to play."

"I thought I could teach you," he said softly, but she'd already left the room.

He turned to Connie who met his unspoken question with a rueful smile.

"She's in pain. There's a lot going on. Can I see?"

DJ passed her the guitar, and she gave it a strum, but with time and transit the tuning had slipped. He reached out his hand, but she said she could do it. He sat back on his heels, watched his sister turn pegs and thumb strings the way he'd taught her, adjusting the intervals till the open chord rang clear.

"It's a beautiful present."

"Story of my life," he said.

"What happened this morning?"

His knees ached as he rose from the floor. "I'm not having a tag sale—I can tell you that much."

Connie rested her hands on the guitar. "Oh-kay."

"I'm just gonna have Goodwill haul the whole mess away."

"*DJ.*"

"I got a headache, I need a cigarette, and I don't want to talk about it, okay? So much fucking talk."

Connie shook her head from side to side. "A second tantrum—very nice." She set the guitar down beside the couch, balancing it the same way he would, with its neck against the upholstered arm. Then she picked up her book, took out the scrap of paper marking her place, and without looking up from the page whose corner she now held between forefinger and thumb, said, "Whatever you say."

Outside, DJ flicked and flicked his lighter, but it wouldn't catch. "*Goddammit,*" he said, the filter pinched between his lips as he walked back into the kitchen and bent over the stove. That clicked and clicked too, but when the flame finally rose, he turned the burner off, went back into the living room, and sat down on the other end of the couch.

"Have you grown up yet?" said Connie. "We're drowning in Motrin, if you want."

"I just need to eat something. What about Elise? She gonna be all right?"

"Well, she's eleven, her arm's in a sling, and her dad—besides taking off—only gives her a gift card, and you, you buy her a glass egg, a great hat, and you give her a guitar. It's a bit of an onslaught."

"I'm such an idiot."

"That's neither here nor there," she said, and DJ smirked. "She's not crazy about me right now, either. I'm just giving her some room to breathe—I'll check in on her in a minute. In the meantime, you wanna tell me your plan? Because I thought we had one."

This was the thing about Connie—she could give you so much shit, but the whole time she'd still be thinking of the best thing to do, vying for a better or fairer solution at every turn. Even growing up—whether hatching a plan to annoy their sisters or divvying up the last of the Easter Peeps and jellybeans—there was a way she'd lean toward you with grand authority and say, *here's what we'll do.* How could he let her down?

DJ told Connie of his own overwhelm, of the cash he hoped to garner from the sale of his records, the Martin, and the rest of the guitars—maybe five thousand dollars in all. He'd give her the money, empty the bigger space, and they could zero out and start over. There were all the books and shelves—more time that he'd wasted moving things around, but he'd only need to bring the bins of Belinda's photos to the basement.

"That can't be all you want to keep."

"No? Weren't you the one asking why I didn't let everything go?"

"I know I said that, but ... " she tsked and sighed. "Has to be something else you can do."

DJ both did and didn't want to hear what she might come up with. His own last-ditch plan had been punishingly satisfying, a deserved bitter brew he felt determined to swallow. But before she could tell him her thoughts, Elise appeared in the living room doorway.

"I don't know what's wrong with me," she said.

"C'mere," said Connie. "It's been a rough week."

Elise eased onto the couch, nestled against her, and closed her eyes. "Can I still keep it?"

"The guitar?" said DJ. "It's yours."

"And you'll still teach me a couple of chords?"

"Absolutely."

Connie smoothed her hand over Elise's forehead, then looked over at DJ, as if to say, *You see?* "Three Little Birds," she said, and when Elise, as though drifting off to sleep, murmured *Three what?* Connie murmured back, *Nothing.* But DJ grinned, catching the reference to Bob Marley's reassuring lyric, the classic reggae beat and lilting melody now running through his head. Maybe not every little thing, but this one little thing would be all right.

"Still your favorite, I hope," Connie said, coming downstairs with two tumblers of amaretto, eager to hash things out after settling Elise in bed. About the money, they went round and round, finally agreeing that she'd take the greater portion from the sale of the Martin, split it between Gretchen and Denise to offset what she owed. DJ would keep whatever he made from the rest—walking-around money, as their mom used to say—to tide him over till he found some kind of part-time work. But her "something else" was a kind of renovation. The smaller storage unit was five by ten, plenty big enough to fit the ping-pong table. DJ could reassemble his shelving, which Connie would then use to store the boxes now resting on and under the ping-pong table, along with anything else DJ wanted to keep—some winter clothes, she prodded, if nothing else. This would clear enough space for him to bring home the bins of photos, along with his real dresser and the Formica table, to use as a desk. Belinda's bedside bookshelf would probably fit, too, and there was room for his nightstand on the far side of the couch. It was strange to hear Connie catalogue his stuff, one item leading to the next as she thought out loud, adding a pair of the vinyl-seated chairs and the standing lamp with the metal shades to his list of potential re-furnishings. Goodwill could cart off the rest, if that remained his intent, and she'd split the monthly bill with him for the smaller unit, which was only sixty-nine bucks. As she ticked off each step of her plan, all DJ could say was okay. Only when she suggested he postpone Goodwill's pick-up did he object—if he didn't do it tomorrow, he might lose his nerve, and then what?

In the end, they determined that she and Elise would

come with him on Sunday for moral support. Over the coming week, while he still had full use of her car, he'd bring over what he could manage himself from the house, and the following weekend she'd help swap out the bigger pieces. They clinked glasses and sipped their mild drinks. Neither of them said how much more sense it would've made if his twenty-five-year-old mattress weren't the only thing he divested himself of when he was still in Brooklyn, or if they'd actually talked about how it might work—his living here—before he arrived.

"I wasn't thinking it would be a permanent thing," Connie said, picking at a spot where the leather piping on the sofa cushion between them was giving way, "or that you'd want it to."

"What'd you think?" he asked, feeling a pleasant warmth from the liqueur. "I don't know—that you'd want to get a studio or something in town. What'd *you* think?"

The look he gave her was sheepish. "I didn't—you know that."

"Right." She ran her hands through her hair, clasped them behind her head. "Well, you may be stuck with the pull-out sofa, but you won't have to live out of a set of cheap plastic drawers." She cast her gaze around the room, settling on the bookshelf directly across from them, where the unframed photo of Belinda rested beside the mended figurine. "At least you'll have some room to put your own stuff. And we should maybe get you a hamper." She tipped her chin in a kind of command, and DJ looked behind him, past the end of the couch, where he'd been piling his dirty clothes. "You can't let this get—"

"I know—I won't. I won't. I promise. A hamper would be good."

"Or you could just walk them to the laundry room. There's a basket in there."

"I can do that."

"You'll have to do your own wash and chip in for food."

"I can do that, too."

"It's not so bad, is it? Living here with me?"

"It has its moments."

Connie scoffed, gathered their glasses, and stood up. "Nothing left then, I suppose."

This last made him uneasy. "How's that?"

"Nothing left but my own shit to sort out."

His pick-up time was a window from two to five, and DJ had fretted about weather and them having to sit for hours by the side of the road like suburban nomads. But Sunday was sunny and warm, and he'd barely rolled up the door before Goodwill arrived. The two men weren't pleased at the time he took to consider each bag and box but remained polite as they loaded the remnants of his former life onto the tailgate, raised and moved it all into the cavernous truck. Connie tipped them each ten bucks—an obvious detail he hadn't considered. That second kiss, the one Andrea had initiated, played through his mind, but more and more like something he'd only imagined.

DJ joined Connie and Elise in the near-empty storage space, which now resembled the spare set of a downtown play—*Remnant Man*, or maybe *The Bureau of David Jasper Edwards*. He opened the two big bags of his clothes, dug out a peacoat, a down parka, a pair of fur earmuffs, plus a classic Burberry scarf which he found appealing, but didn't recognize. There were any number of lightweight jackets, pilling sweaters, and a couple of vintage suits—nothing he could imagine wanting to store or put on again, rifling through it all as easily as he might a flea market rack. *Yes, no, no, no, no, no.* The only thing that caught at his heart was a worn pair of Beatle boots—he'd have been sad not to have rescued those. Beyond that, he

153

kept only the few boxes labeled TCHOTCHKES with their hyphenated room source, and one that read KITCHEN—DECALED GLASSES.

"What are those for?" asked Elise, and he was grateful not to hear the rattle of broken glass when he picked it up.

More than any singular history—though he did remember how he'd gotten or been given each one—these were juice-size and taller glasses that he'd always loved, accumulated over the years. One with Hulk Hogan, a couple of Flintstones jelly jars, a lowball glass with a wide-eyed owl. Others had patterns of flowers or stripes—there'd been a zombie glass with a leopard print, though that one had shattered in an unfortunate landslide of dirty dishes. Belinda had been keen on one from the Seattle World's Fair. A dozen or so, treasured for their whimsy, the feeling of them in your hand.

"Just regular drinking glasses," he said, "but with funny or cool designs."

Elise nodded, then she said, "Can I see the records before we go?"

He looked at Connie, who seemed equally surprised.

"It's okay with me," she said.

The three of them walked around to the side of the building and DJ opened the lock, then slowly rolled up the smaller green door.

"*Wow*," said Elise and Connie in unison.

"Yeah," DJ said. "I know."

Elise asked if he'd found the record Andrea wanted and he shook his head.

"Can I have one?"

"If you want." He looked at Connie, whose shrug said, *Your guess is as good as mine.*

Elise circled each double row of records, then stood between them and closed her eyes as though making a wish. DJ's hand rose to his chest, his heart banging its old song of grief and tenderness. Then Elise opened her eyes and bent down, cautious of her arm in its bright blue sling. She ran her index finger across the thin spines, stopping midway to draw one out. "*Rumours*," she said, flipping the cover around to the front. "Fleetwood Mac. Is this good?"

"*Yes,*" he said, now in unison with Connie, and they both broke up.

"Excellent choice," he said, the words ringing in his ears. In a world where decisions were made all around her, albeit with her interests at heart, maybe letting her choose, even blindly, was the greater gift. DJ was struck with an odd memory. There'd been some kind of a yearly fair with games at their elementary school, though he couldn't imagine what occasioned such a thing. Even stranger was the game that repeatedly drew him. A deep tray would be filled with sawdust, and there was a sieve-like scoop, and for whatever number of red paper tickets, you were allowed a single scoop with the chance of gathering a coin. Not even a quarter, but dimes, pennies, and nickels. Why that sieve in his hand, the feathery feel of the sawdust, had given him such a pleasurable sense of hope and luck, he couldn't say. As though he'd been panning for gold.

"Deej?" said Connie. "You okay?"

"Yeah, yeah. Shall we go?"

It was only as they drove away that DJ looked back and thought, *all gone.*

The next morning was pure lion, the lamb disappeared, and DJ drove over to the storage unit early. Box by box, he slid the two rows of records farther back from the door, neither the blustery rain nor this slight retraction boding well. But Alex's guy, a fit and affable man named

Rob, appeared exactly on time, dashing from a white cargo van and under the partly rolled-up door, wearing the kind of turquoise zip-up jacket that made DJ think of mountaineers.

"Quite a haul you've got here," he said, then began randomly picking out albums, removing them from cover and inner sleeve to inspect for damage. "Decent shape, generally. This all the classical?" he said of the crates and DJ nodded. "Any way you would categorize the rest?"

"Fairly spread across the genres, with a heavy emphasis on the jingly-jangly sound of '80s guitar."

Rob smiled. "You play?"

"Some," said DJ.

"More sentimental than collectible value?"

"Should be a few things that'll get a fair price."

"But?"

DJ looked down at the boxes. "I couldn't tell you where they are."

"You leaving town?"

"Returning."

The look Rob gave him was perplexed. He squinted at the rows and DJ couldn't tell if he was calculating profit or considering whether it was worth his while to take them at all.

"You'd do better if you had a full catalogue."

"I know."

Rob held his hand to his chin, a finger resting across his mouth as he tipped his head back and forth, the tempo of the rain picking up. For the hundredth time, DJ thought of Tracy, and all the effort she'd spent. Then he thought of Barbara Eden in *I Dream of Jeannie*, of Elizabeth Montgomery in *Bewitched*, wishing he could wrinkle or twitch his nose to make the crates and cartons, Rob in his too vivid jacket—maybe even himself—disappear. Only he didn't really want to vanish; he just wanted to leap ahead to some unseeable future when this painful passage and all its losses would have long slipped away.

"Four-fifty for the lot," Rob said.

"Done," said DJ, the exchange seeming backwards to him, like his foolish negotiation with Andrea over a paperweight.

He raised the door the rest of the way up and began re-taping while Rob backed up the van. Once they'd loaded everything, Rob counted bills out into his hand just the way DJ had first imagined, told him to tell Alex hello, and wished him good luck. The wheels of the van ground in the gravel but then took hold, and Rob drove slowly forward, then turned onto the blacktop.

DJ pulled the door down far enough to let in some light but keep out the rain. He knew he should start building the shelves—he had a couple of hours before picking up Elise—but he was finding it hard to breathe. He sat down on the cold concrete and bent his head to his knees. It was as though the sound of the rain was inside his skull and with it Belinda's voice, soft and hushing, *That's enough, now. You're all right, you're all right, you're all right.*

The cash in his pocket was like a taunt, and as DJ picked up a carton of Winstons and a black-and-white golf-sized umbrella in Kingston Plaza, he tried not to think of the money he'd spent to acquire all those records and whether it had equaled the pleasure they'd brought. Even if his circumstances were different, music was no longer the physical ritual it had once been; ironic—he saw that—to buy Connie a record player when he was selling his whole damn collection. For the same money he could've gotten her a little Jam speaker, played any music she wanted from his iPad, his phone. *For the same money,* like a song in high rotation, the recurring strain of his life.

It was just as this notion was fluttering about in his brain that DJ noticed the pinball machine in the back of the shop. Four Aces. A game that once held a high place, in the college bar he and his circle had favored, and in the Times Square arcade that he'd guiltily haunted his first years in New York, stopping off on his way home from or arriving late to mind-numbing shifts as a copy editor in the cavernous libraries of law firms.

"You can play, if you want," said the cashier. "Handed down from my uncle, but I'm trying to sell."

"How much?"

"Six hundred."

"The magic number."

"Say what?"

DJ walked over to the machine, rested his hands on the corners of the apron. Before him the familiar bumpers and lanes, the scoreboard with its bawdy depiction of four women in high-heeled boots, aces of each suit looming above their heads like a row of monuments. His strange aversion for the number four the thing that had led him to conquer the game.

"Out of my league," he said, turning back to the cashier.

The man held out a handful of quarters. "Knock yourself out anyway."

The first flicker and ping of the machine coming to life sent a warmth down DJ's wrists, a subtle vibration at the center of his palms as he clicked the flippers. Oh, yes. He had missed this! He pulled back the plunger to release the ball. *Ding, ding, ding. Fuck the right thing.*

You weren't supposed to leave your car unattended in the line at Elise's school, but DJ spoke with one of the day's crossing guards, obtaining permission to meet Elise at the door. It wasn't that things were awkward between them since she'd gotten hurt, but they were off-kilter, skewed where they'd previously, if cautiously, aligned, the Yamaha left leaning against the arm of the living room couch. Two to three weeks, the orthopedist had told Connie, before she could take off the sling. DJ wondered how she'd maneuvered through her day at school, about her recently absented best friend, and whether there was anyone else in her class to whom she'd have told the story. When a space like that opened up in middle school, he knew, it was unlikely to be filled.

Buffeted about as kids burst through the doors, DJ held his new umbrella high, scanning side to side for Elise, his heart thudding nervously as the crowd thinned out. But Elise had merely waited for the rush to die down, the top loop of her backpack firmly grasped in her right hand, her classic yellow slicker donned like a cape over her head and shoulders. Like four ducklings, he and his sisters had had coats like that.

"*E.*," he said lightly.

"Oh, hey," she said, momentarily unguarded as he shifted his umbrella to cover them both. Then she looked down at the wet steps as though steadying her nerve. "Who'd you bribe?" she said, a mumble he almost didn't hear.

She moved ahead and he followed a step behind, only thinking to take her bag after they'd reached the sidewalk. She declined but let him open the door for her when they got to the car.

"How'd you manage?" he asked, the drivers who'd been lined up behind them now steering around their parked car with pointed honks of complaint.

"Not great," she said. "You?"

With a small huff of a laugh, he admitted the same.

She seemed about to say something, then changed her mind. "Can we go?"

"Of course," he said, and started the car, the wipers

taking up their squeaking rhythm. He tried to pull out, but it was as if the other drivers had made a pact not to let him in.

The rest of the week was much the same: storage unit in the morning, Elise in the afternoon, with the addition of Connie working late to make up for the days she took off. On Tuesday, he'd had to go back to Home Depot for a rubber mallet to assemble the Metro shelves, and on Wednesday he stopped by the antiques store. To ask if he could hang on to the hand truck, to deliver his own white envelope, containing Alex's ten percent, and to bear the disappointing news about Andrea's record.

"*Ohh*," she said, elbows on the counter, chin sunk into her hands, as he described opening the boxes and the dismantling of his quixotic arrangement. In his mind's eye, he told her, he could still reach out his hand to the section where it was likely to be. He didn't say anything about her not calling and neither did she. Andrea tucked the envelope into Alex's datebook, asked if he'd at least gotten a fair deal.

"Less than I hoped for, more than I expected."

"So not entirely terrible."

"One way to see it." Maybe not the album she wanted, but he could've found something she'd like—why didn't he? "How's your sister-in-law holding up?"

"Alex wants her to see a shrink, but Molly says she won't take meds."

"And the baby?"

"*Alicia*," she said. "Cute, but her vote's undecided."

So taken with the way she'd lit up at the baby's name, DJ nearly missed the joke. "Good one," he said, a beat late.

She looked at him curiously. "You all right?"

"People keep asking me that. What about you?" He ran

his hand along the edge of the counter. "Going back to Park Slope?"

"I'm gonna have to, eventually. I do have my own life." She seemed to catch herself here but went on. "And Alex ... well—family. *You* know. I suppose I owe him." She patted her arm. "How's Elise?"

"Sprained, but not broken."

"I heard David left."

"You did?"

"I made a small chandelier for the baby's room. He was supposed to help me hang it."

"*Oh*," he said, wrenched by a sudden thought. He scanned her face. "Were you ..."

"Me and David? God—no. That'd be bizarre—I wouldn't have—"

"Right—sorry—of course you wouldn't." The pain of his mistake squeezed at his ribs, his head. "Everything's just been so ..." DJ looked at her, a plea. "I don't even know."

"It's all right," she said, adding her own apologetic frown, and he knew what was coming wasn't good. "But there is someone—or there was. There may be—I don't know. I had to come up here. It's ..." Her hand rose and then fell again as she shook her head.

"A situation?"

The half-laugh she let out was harsh. "A situation—yeah."

Looming above her, the giant Coca-Cola clock emitted a loud click he'd never noticed, as the second hand swept past twelve.

"*That's* annoying," he said, and she followed his gaze to the clock.

"You've no idea."

"Well," he said, "I really should get going."

She smiled at his use of her line, but her expression was wistful. "I'm sorry if I gave you the wrong idea. I should never have—"

"No, no," he said, waving her off. "I just have to pick up Elise."

"Alex has another hand truck somewhere—keep that one as long as you need."

"Great—thanks." DJ scrambled for a handhold. That second kiss—the one she'd started—might be a wash, but her status remained uncertain, pining his most familiar state, and he could sure as hell do with a friend. "We could still have a coffee sometime, couldn't we? I'd love to go back to that place by the Rondout."

"Sometime," she said, "sure—it's just hard to know how long—"

"No—I know—"

"Or when—"

"Of course," he said, his disappointment growing harder to contain.

"Maybe Monday, though?"

"*Oh*—okay, yeah. that could work." *Oh—okay yeah?* Very smooth.

"I'll call you," she said.

Already deep in imagining this rendezvous, DJ was halfway to Connie's before he realized that she'd said that before, and that by Monday he'd no longer have a car.

Because Connie came downstairs each night, eager for his progress, DJ was compelled to follow through with her plan. He'd half enjoyed hammering away at the Metro shelves and, to assuage one morning's anxiety, had even slid a few of the heaviest cartons onto the lowest level. It was Belinda's fine art books and museum catalogs, some-where among them, that had kept him from sending the whole batch off with Goodwill—as though, besides her photos, carelessly dispensing with her books would be the one thing she'd object to.

More and more, DJ's memories returned him to their earliest days, with Belinda new to the city and he her guide to both its renowned and hidden treasures. Belinda with a camera around her neck, their hands clasped together in the pocket of her wool coat, November's wind whipping their faces raw until they ducked into the Hungarian pastry place up by St. John the Divine. He'd spent half his life in cafés poring over menus, ordering cups of coffee for the women he loved or hoped to.

In the miles and miles that he'd walked with his wife down city streets, equally prized with their favorite spots—the pocket parks and river views; the thrift and antiques stores in their neighborhood; the three-star restaurants and corner joints; the book, record, and clothing stores across two boroughs—was the pleasure of discovering something overlooked, the joy of something new. Amidst all the life going on around them—buildings going up, being restored, or torn down; an endless variety of people seated at nearby tables or walking, biking, cabbing by—each small detail pointed out, each delicious dish they shared, binding them closer together, weaving a fabric of us. This is what we like, we love, we choose. This is who we are. What would he find that could possibly compare?

Holed up in the crumbling chaos of his Brooklyn apartment, with no one else's concerns but his own, he'd been able to indulge, every now and then, not in a fantasy per se, but in a subtle imagining that Belinda was still with him, was still alive, in any number of incarnations of her younger self—just in another room. He couldn't do it deliberately; it didn't work like that. The moment would arrive of its own accord, a sense of peacefulness mixed with a pleasurable bass note of anticipation.

If he didn't pay it too much attention, if he was able to let that light wash of feeling be, it was as though he could slip, for a few comforting seconds, into an earlier time. Belinda not dead, or even sick, but merely in the kitchen putting water on to boil. Belinda in their bedroom, standing before their closet with its janky door, trying to decide between two summer dresses. Their narrow bathroom filled with steam as she stepped from the shower, wrapped herself in the turquoise-and-white-striped towel she claimed the softest, while he, not ten steps down the hall, would be setting the needle down to "Daydream Believer," one of her all-time favorites. Or passing through the doorway forever half-curtained with her dry cleaning, on his way to the living room to assemble a perfect playlist, download something new. Curating the soundtrack, the bed of music beneath their lives.

There was always the grief that lay in waiting, attached to a particular lyric, a melody—he'd indulged in that clean release, too. But this was something else, a revival of her physical self, a body memory, a residual essence billowing into form. His desire reaching of its own volition through space and time. And it wasn't always music that brought it on.

The first time it happened, he'd been digging through the scarves and hats they stored in a low cedar dresser in the hall, looking for the match to either of two single gloves. Once he'd been clipping his toenails. It was the *ordinariness,* the habitual contours of their days and nights, a flipbook of repeated actions sourced from a million frames, the two figures aging across the riffling pages.

There was no particular moment that he wanted back. He wanted any one of them—he wanted them all. He had not paid close enough attention, had not considered that any more could be lost, and now here he was, driving back and forth through Hurley, the rooms he and Belinda had filled finally repainted, the plumbing repaired, the ceiling replastered, their home taken up with other people's lives. *Belinda.* For all he knew, the entire building had been torn down. Being here, in the place he'd come from, he didn't know who he was.

10

By Friday, the ping-pong table was cleared, above and below, and DJ laid out the small trove of boxes he'd saved. Had he gotten rid of the chifforobe when Sarah wanted him to, had he and Belinda never dragged it up from the street to begin with, it would never have knocked down Elise, and when she came home from school, they could've played a last game or two before putting the table in storage. He sighed, not at the thought of them playing—or his pointless furniture remorse—but at the idea of himself stored here in his little sister's basement. Connie was bound to be annoyed at his using the table when he'd just have to clear it again, but it was his time to spend and, once he opened these last few boxes, he might as well break them down and toss the packing material.

He began with the box containing the ukulele, first turning it on its side to work out the tune. He could read music, but couldn't hear the notes in his head just by looking at them, so he brought over his iPad and opened the virtual piano app. Expecting something obscure, DJ was surprised by the melody he played, harking back to the occasion of her gift. *Happy birthday to you.*

Tracy was moving to California for the foreseeable future—there was no need to tell of the storage space fiasco or his impulsive and final dispersal of the apartment-full of things she'd spent days packing. When his call went to voicemail, he simply said, "I just got your musical message. And I love you, by the way."

He'd forgotten what a charming thing the ukulele was to behold. Its pale green a whimsical and cheering shade, the tail piece shaped like a shark, denoting its line within the Kala brand, and a Hawaiian flavor. *Kala*, when he looked it up, was defined as a verb: to loosen, untie, free, release, unburden, absolve. He had to laugh at that, a hidden message within the gift and a bit of trivia he doubted Tracy would've been aware of.

DJ snapped a few air pockets of the bubble wrap, laid the uke on the couch, and set the box labeled MIXED ROOMS—BELINDA ART on the ping-pong table, then decided he would save that one, maybe open it with Elise—his box of boxes. He unpacked the rest of the cartons, a kind of panic overtaking him as he went through the last one, though he couldn't have said what he was looking for until he found it. Cushioned by packing peanuts, the celadon teapot of the bearded man and his deer. He would rearrange, once they'd moved his furniture in, but for now he set it in the middle of Connie's shelves, alongside the unframed photo of Belinda and the dancing figurine.

Before he picked up Elise, DJ drove back to the more dilapidated side of Kingston where he and David had encountered Ryan. After getting turned around in a disconcerting series of one-way streets, he managed to backtrack onto Broadway, once again passing a sketchy string of hotdog joints and empty storefronts, until he reached the music store of his youth. Unlike the pair of trendy guitar shops in the Stockade District that drew both tourists and professional musicians, Rimaldi's Music had always served a more general clientele, renting everything from accordions to tubas, selling sheet music and songbooks, and a few decent guitars.

Above the familiar red brick, bars had been installed across the high windows that still bore the store's name in a curling gold script, and the heavy grate on the door made it look more like a pawn shop now. He had to be buzzed in, but the glittering array of brass instruments still hung from the ceiling, violins still lined the back wall above the drum kits, and there was still the same smattering of electric and acoustic guitars. Only the song titles in the music racks had changed, giving rise to a mix of pleasure and grief.

A well-built man in his forties stood behind the counter, sporting the same long denim apron DJ remembered as the owner's signature style. He held a grimy polishing cloth in his hand, a trio of velvet-lined cases open before him, displaying two flutes and a soprano sax.

"The public school bands—they're the worst. You'd think they were dipping their hands in Slurpee. How can I help you today?"

"I was always partial to the blue raspberry myself." DJ checked the price of a Beatles songbook, then slid it back into the rack. He'd driven here with the notion of asking for a job. Moving up to the counter he said, "I used to come in here when I was a kid. I bought my first guitar from Mr. Rimaldi."

"That was my dad. I run this place with my wife now, and my eldest—that's his picture there—he helps out on the weekends, like I did."

DJ looked up at the wall, where an eight-by-ten glossy showed a young man in a red plaid shirt holding a sunburst Epiphone guitar. They resembled each other, but not the kindly, silver-haired man he recalled.

"So, your father…"

He snapped the case closed on the sax. "Heart attack. Years ago."

"*Oh*," said DJ. He felt lost in time, a wandering ghost. "I'm sorry to hear that."

The man set the cloth aside and wiped his hands down the front of his apron. "I've got an Ovation with a lovely round sound, if you're in the market for something new."

DJ curled his fingers into fists; if he picked up the guitar there was a good chance he'd buy it. "Nah. I was just passing through."

The man nodded and took up his cloth. "A sentimental journey."

"Something like that."

"Well, let me know if you change your mind."

DJ turned back toward the music racks and picked out a laminated chord chart for Elise. It only cost a couple of bucks and he wouldn't make it a present, wouldn't even show it to her till she had full use of her arm. It'd be his—just something he had around that she could use as a reference. Once he'd paid, the man's attention returned to the flutes. There was no work for DJ here, and he left the shop without saying goodbye.

In the car, DJ wrapped his fingers around the wheel and let his head fall forward. He was nowhere cool enough, or a good enough musician, to be hired at those trendier guitar stores. His last job, as a manager at the Borders in Union Square, was one he'd mostly hated, cursed by association to those first terrifying days of Belinda's diagnosis. He'd been friends with a few people there, which helped him stick it out for a while, but it had been a relief to give notice and leave them behind, any notion of work falling away once he was caring for Belinda full time. And now? Now he was nothing more than an old and foolish man, tethered to the earth by a handful of kitschy objects. He kept trying to go back because he couldn't see anything lying ahead.

DJ let his hands drop and sat back, slow to note the hour on a defunct bank's corner clock as he watched the passing trucks and cars. "Shit," he said. "*Shit, shit, shit.*"

He'd be at the end of the line, but if he took 213 and cut over to Washington, he might still be on time for Elise.

The pick-up line was already inching forward, kids buckled into the rest of their afternoon, DJ's phone ringing as he pulled in. He imagined the school having called Connie, and Connie calling him now, wondering where the fuck he was.

"*Hey*," he said, doubly relieved to find Andrea on the other end of the line. He'd begun to think she wouldn't call. This was the last day he'd be picking up Elise—he could see her now, trudging toward the car. Being late was bad enough—he didn't want to be on the phone. "Can I call you back in a little while?"

"If you say yes first—I'm kind of in a jam and technically you owe me."

He got out of the car to open the rear door, mouthed the word *sorry*. Elise hefted her bag onto the seat, then shooed him off and let herself in the front.

"Yes to what?" he said, and Andrea explained that she had to go back to the city on Saturday, that she wanted to ask Alex to let DJ cover for her at the store.

"It's more of a favor to me, but he'll pay you."

DJ slid back into the driver's seat. A boon—a bone being tossed his way from an unexpected quarter, when he had no option left. They were supposed to swap the ping-pong table for his furniture on Saturday—but there was always Sunday. Connie would of course be thrilled, and he was glad Andrea had thought of him—just not exactly this way.

"Your situation?" he asked.

"Work, actually."

Was it chandeliers? Or did she do something else? He knew so little about Andrea, wanted to ask her more. Did she even remember their prospective coffee date? He held up a finger, begging one more minute from Elise, the look she gave him piqued. "I've gotta check with my sister, but probably yes."

"This is my cell. Call me soon as you know."

She hung up without saying goodbye, and yet a ripple of optimism ran through his dismay. She did call, necessity aside. And filling in at the store felt like an ongoing connection. One bound by more than hasty kisses or his randomly dropping by, even if it meant she'd be back in Brooklyn for however long. It wasn't as if she were leaving for Antarctica, and he felt something close to a certainty that this was a start and not an end.

DJ had been last in the pick-up line. In the delay of his phone call, a wide gap had spread between their car and the rest, but once he pulled up it would still be a long slow exit.

"Sorry 'bout that," he said to Elise.

She opened and closed her right hand like a yakking puppet, and he couldn't tell whether the gesture mocked his chatting on the phone or his apology.

"Screw the line," he said, and put the car in reverse. The Civic made an awful whirring, Elise braced her hand against the dash, and one of the crossing guards blew a whistle. But by the time they'd cleared the school building and fenced-in yard, they were both whooping and laughing as he screeched into the street.

"*So there*," he said, and with a nod Elise echoed his words.

When it came to Connie, it was best to ask and not presume, but she was back-slappingly delighted by the prospect of his working at Alex's store, unconcerned about postponing their furniture swap till Sunday. "It's just the one day," he warned, not wanting her enthusiasm to jinx what he hoped would lead to more. Work was the crucial thing to Connie, a sign he was keeping—at least for now—the promises he'd made. But his sights were still set on Andrea. Any song, any movie, any story that mattered, was always about the girl, and DJ showed up at the store with two lattes, offering her the choice of blueberry muffin or orange-cranberry scone.

"You're a life saver," she said, and jokes he thought better of making skittered through his brain, as she took the scone but turned down the latte.

"Already up to the gills with caffeine," she said, calling to mind the trio of animal teapots he and Elise had admired. There was a quip in there, too, but Andrea seemed harried and pressed for time, hastily running him through Alex's system of receipts, the quirk of the register drawer.

"Thing'll slam right into you. Any questions?"

"What are you gonna be doing?" he asked. A last attempt to keep her.

"In the city? I didn't say?"

"You did not."

"Wow. Okay. That just goes to show, doesn't it?"

He nodded, though he'd no idea what it showed, and then she told him she worked for a food stylist on a freelance basis, her weekend to be spent shopping at Fairway and Whole Foods, prepping and organizing what she could in advance of a three-day shoot.

"Sounds hectic. The opposite of here." He meant upstate in general, but she took him literally.

"Not on Saturday—you'll see," She bit into the scone as if for punctuation. "*Mmm—good*," she said, then reached for the latte and took a gulp. "Guess I'm taking this after all. We're okay, right?"

Okay wasn't half of what he wanted, but before he could answer, the neon of the Coca-Cola clock flickered and they both looked up.

"That fucking thing. I hope it's a good day. I really do have to go."

Throughout the morning and early afternoon, a steady trickle of customers came into the store, day-trippers and other weekend passers-through-town, looking to bring home some small token of their visit, a solid trace of an earlier life to mark an afternoon in their own. DJ sold a set of shot glasses with worn gold rims, a carved wooden box circa 1972, a child's wooden chair someone had painted a trendy robin's-egg blue, and four coasters he wouldn't have minded keeping for himself. Made of thin cork, they were decorated along one side with a series of narrow black and white rectangles arranged like the keys on a piano and, within the rest of the square, a random array of musical notes circling a large calligraphic rendering of a treble clef.

Andrea aside, he was more comfortable here with these worn objects and their associations—or lack thereof—than he imagined he'd be in any bookstore, surrounded by the shelves and shelves of books representing the world's accomplishments. There was, of course, a token number of books in a corner of Alex's store, but these were classic tomes, favored more for their bindings and editions than the content they held, and kept in a locked glass case, to be viewed only upon request—according to a filigreed card whose advisory had *not* been written in Sharpie. Surprising among them was an original hardcover copy of *Stuart Little*, with Garth Williams's illustration of E.B. White's tender-hearted mouse, paddling his birch bark canoe down a leaf-lined river, the words SUMMER MEMORIES inscribed on its bow. A book he hadn't read since he was a kid, but whose pages he'd once turned to again and again, until the characters had seemed his own familiars—creatures he found himself missing each time their stories came to a close, their lives carrying on somewhere in the ether without him, as he, too, searched for his own Margalo.

Toward the end—when she became too fatigued to hold up a book, the type swimming before her eyes—he'd sometimes read to Belinda. Though it was the sound of his voice, he believed, that had soothed and buoyed her through those difficult hours more than any words on the page.

DJ wiped the screen of his mind, ran a soundtrack of The La's, and called up a summer weekend, early in their marriage, that they spent with friends who'd rented a house on Fire Island. He'd been reading *Dune,* and as they sat in low nylon chairs, borrowed beach towels draped over their white legs, the ocean wide and sparkling before them, Belinda picked up the thick paperback, opened to the page where he'd folded the corner down, and began reading to him aloud. All he remembered of the book was that Kyle MacLachlan had starred in the movie version, but he could clearly see his wife's long delicate fingers as they turned a page, pushed her round wire-rimmed glasses up her nose, could smell the exquisite combination of salt, sweat, and suntan lotion on her skin.

How young they'd been, a small pile of shells gathered on the sand between them; Belinda partial to the translucent peach and gold tones of the ones she called mermaid's toenails. He'd never asked, hadn't wanted to know, if that was the name they really went by, preferring to think she'd made it up. His own mermaid girl, deep below the ocean waves now.

At the creak of the door, DJ expected yet another stranger, but found himself looking into Tracy's grinning face.

"Holy shit," he said. "What the hell are you doing here?"

"I sold the Martin to a guy in New Paltz. Then I went by the house—nice place, by the way—and Connie told me where to find you. *Don't cry,* for God's sake."

"I'm just glad to see you—I can't believe you're here."

"Only for an hour or so."

He came out from behind the counter and as they hugged all DJ could think was *don't go.*

When they pulled apart, Tracy glanced around the store. "Looks like you've landed in the perfect spot."

"I'm just filling in for the woman who works here, and even she—it's her brother's place." He tried to think of what he did and didn't want to say. "It's a little complicated."

"And what's complicated's name?"

DJ felt himself blush. "How do you do that?"

"How long have I known you?"

"Andrea."

Tracy picked up a Peanuts lunchbox, smiled at the clink of its metal handle as she zigged it back and forth, touched her finger to the figure of Schroeder bent over the keys of his little toy piano, then set it back down. "It's a good name."

"What does that even mean?"

She laughed. "I don't know. It means I hope it gets uncomplicated."

"You look good," he said. "Still have your heart set on L.A.?" The words came out flip and her expression darkened.

"It's not a *whim*. People move, people change all the time."

"Not me."

"But you already have—maybe not willingly, but still."

Gazing past the window display, DJ looked into the street, and though it wasn't parked in sight, he imagined just walking out the door and getting into Tracy's old Buick wagon with its wooden sides—a boat of a car you could never find a parking spot for on a Brooklyn street. Imagined driving and driving, every vista, every day, brand new, all the way to California. To a place without winter, with no stuff of his own, where he might be, or at least become someone else.

"That's quite the clock," she said, breaking the strained silence between them.

DJ glanced up, then smiled at Tracy, sadness spreading like a liquid heat through his chest. "It's the real thing."

"Why don't I go get us some coffee and we'll settle up." She patted the leather mini backpack slung over her shoulder. "I think you're gonna be happy."

Tracy, as ever, had done well by him, bringing his grand total, including the records, closer to six thousand than five. DJ was startled when she handed him a pair of checks and not the envelope of cash that had come to seem the customary method of exchange since he'd been back in Hurley. The larger one was a bank check for the Martin, the other her personal check for the rest of his guitars. *For the same money,* he almost said out loud, he could stake himself somewhere else—near Tracy in Los Angeles, near Andrea someplace in Brooklyn, if not Park Slope. Though, obviously, he wouldn't be able to sustain it. This conversion of his stuff into money, his arrangement with Connie, was the best and only move he could make.

It was more than he'd gotten for the Martin, but he would give Connie four thousand dollars, no matter what she said, making for a tidy split of two each for Gretchen and Denise.

He picked up the lunchbox Tracy had admired earlier. *$45* the price tag read. "Take it—you know you want to. On me."

"*DJ,*" she said, putting a hand to his cheek. "Thank you. But no."

"So, this is it, then."

"For now."

"I'm off at five—you could stay for dinner."

"I have to get back. I should've left a half hour ago."

175

He walked her to the door, held it open for her.

Tracy inhaled deeply. "God, it smells good up here, doesn't it? Like spring."

His heart was racing, his hands beginning to sweat. "How do I even thank you?"

"You can't," she said, and then, as they hugged one last time, "I miss her, too."

"Well," said DJ, when they finally broke apart. "I guess I'll see ya."

"Down the line."

"Down the elevator."

"You'll be okay. We both will," she added, and he hoped it would be true.

From the doorway, he leaned into the street, watched her weave through the sidewalk traffic of Saturday shoppers. At the corner, Tracy looked back and waved, then she turned and disappeared from view.

It wasn't long before Alex eased open the door, a finger to his lips, the baby asleep in the car seat hooked over his arm. He set the car seat on the counter, the diaper bag on the floor, and tucked in the blanket, pink with little white stars, around the baby's feet. In a little do-si-do he and DJ swapped places.

Alex flipped through the receipts. "Not a terrible afternoon," he said, keeping his voice low, and DJ had the sense he meant more than the numbers. Bracing his hand against the drawer so it wouldn't bang, Alex opened the register, counted out four twenties, slid them across the counter.

"Assuming the rest adds up, I've got an estate sale I'd like to schedule for next Saturday. Same deal if you'd want to come in."

"That'd be good." DJ wondered what this meant about Andrea's return and braced in his own way for the all-too-familiar feeling of being trapped. But all he felt was the release of being done for the day; the promise of more work, along with Tracy's checks, like a prize to bring home to Connie.

The baby stirred and Alex lifted her free of the car seat, her cheeks flushed from sleep, her eyes drawn to his face as he settled her in the crook of his arm.

"Hello, my beautiful girl," he said, and the baby cooed. "Let's get you changed. Would you like that? Yes, you would."

"I'll see you next week then," said DJ, but Alex, busy laying a changing pad across the counter, hadn't seemed to hear, and he'd left, gently closing the door behind him.

Spearing up a green bean at dinner, Connie said, "Well, tomorrow's the day," and DJ understood this was the true beginning, his real moving in. The preceding weeks a re-shuffling dispersal, a shaking out of their lives into this current configuration. Not an errant uncle, a displaced brother crashing in his little sister's basement, in a separate world, but the three of them bound together—he, Connie, and Elise. Homework done, meals made or ordered in, laundry folded, the garbage taken out.

"Maybe next weekend," she went on, "if the weather's nice, we'll just drive right past Catskill Park Storage all the way to the lake. Or go see a movie. Do something fun for a change."

"That'd be nice," he said, "but I'll be working at the store again on Saturday."

"Really? That's great—Sunday then. What do you say, Lisey?"

"Sounds okay."

"Don't everybody jump out of their seats."

"Do we have to go anywhere?" asked Elise.

Connie set down her fork. "You're right. It's been a lot

of running around. I just thought—well, it doesn't matter. *So*," she said to DJ, still looking to lodge her enthusiasm somewhere. "Is this a permanent thing? How's Andrea? How's her sister-in-law doing?"

Each question unsettled DJ a little more. "Could be. Andrea's back in Brooklyn. I did see the baby," he said, trying to give her something. "But only with Alex—I didn't ask."

"Well, it must've been nice to see Tracy at least."

This wasn't at all the way he'd thought this conversation would go—everything felt off, the relief and even pride he'd felt earlier, nowhere to be found. "She sold the guitars."

"Wow—that was fast. That's good news, though, isn't it?"

"Did I tell you she's moving to L.A.?"

"DJ?"

He suddenly found himself standing, his legs unsteady beneath him, though he didn't remember getting up. "I think…" he started to say, then he was racing down the hall to the bathroom, where he promptly threw up.

"Not too dramatic," he said, when Connie came to check on him later. Were he allowed to smoke in the basement, he'd be plowing his way through a pack. Instead, he'd been lying on the couch with the cowboy flannel of Elise's sleeping bag pulled up to his chin, thinking of the blood vessel that had burst in his brain, and the way some people, other people, could rise above, find the phoenix in the ashes. He'd thought Sarah might be that and been twice disappointed. Tracy wasn't leaving *him,* but she was leaving him behind. Moving forward while he remained lodged in tar, a dinosaur of his day.

Lucky, everyone said of his surviving the aneurysm. For DJ, it was more like … getting knocked out the first time you step into the ring. He'd been passive before but had come into a moment of belief in his own possibilities—only to be promptly stricken down. Not so much a punishment (though, maybe, in a way), as a voice saying, *Yeah, buddy—not for you.* He lost his momentum—his tiny epoch of hope—and the will to strive for anything on a larger scale, stumbling through life the same as always, letting others take care of him and steer his course. Only with those temporal blackouts, had it seemed something physical, of a calamitous nature, could happen again. Like his time could so easily run out. *Ding, ding, ding.* But what could you do?

After the aneurysm, his doctor had prescribed a few months' worth of anti-seizure meds and told him not to smoke, which he'd held to, only briefly resuming with the onset of the blackouts. Half to cope with the fear and anxiety, half figuring he was gonna die anyway. Then he didn't. Belinda did. And he started smoking again, beyond the pleasure, as a kind of defiance, even a temptation of death. *Come and get me, motherfucker*, he'd think lighting up, imagining death—hood thrown back, scythe slack at his side—rolling his eyes in exasperation and waving him on with his skeletal hand. *Go. Live. Whatever. My bad.*

"It's a lot," Connie said, standing over the coffee table, where he'd moved the decal glasses and some of the smaller ephemera from his Brooklyn days.

"Looks like a little to me."

"You can never be serious, can you?"

"Does it get more serious than puking?"

Connie tried to frown but couldn't hold it. "Heart attack?"

"Stroke—but I've already had one."

She wedged herself into the bit of couch left at his feet. "You'll feel better once we bring down your furniture and you have somewhere to put the stuff you saved." She studied her shelves. "I could probably put a row's worth of my books in storage, give you a little more room."

"I don't know. I'm kind of used to the way it is. It's been a lot for you, too. I nearly broke your kid's arm, among other things."

"Eh, she has two." Connie clamped a hand to her mouth. "Oh, my God—that's not even funny."

"Kinda was."

"Coked-up dad, divorce, that fucking chifforobe—she's gonna be in therapy forever. I'm a terrible mom."

"You're not—that's the thing. Our parents knew nothing about us, and you … you're really a part of her life."

"And now you are, too."

"Thank you—really. For taking me in, for putting up with me."

"You are a royal pain."

"So I'm told," he said. "So I'm told."

Connie picked up the Hulk Hogan, then set it down with an appreciative *hmm*. "Whatever happened to him?"

"Still around, I think."

She squeezed his foot through the thick sleeping bag. "I gotta get some rest." Halfway up the stairs, she looked back down between the railings. "And tomorrow, Jerome?"

"Yes, Constance?"

"Whatever you do, don't throw up in my car."

They were making the next to last run from the storage unit, the drawers in the back seat of Connie's Civic, the rest of his old wooden dresser bungeed into the trunk, DJ blithely following as she drove the Focus a different route home, passing by the house that she'd shared with David. Maybe Elise had asked, he was thinking, when Connie suddenly braked and pulled over to the curb. He'd seen it too, though it hadn't fully registered. A woman sitting on the half-restored steps, playing with a little girl, a stroller and an old-fashioned doll carriage, on the porch above them, just beside the front door.

DJ had to park farther up the street. He hurried past the Focus, where Elise held her good hand palm up and shook her head. *Fucking David,* he thought, and then, with a panicky feeling, called out for Connie to wait up.

Either she didn't hear or she didn't care. DJ saw the woman pick up the little girl and call to someone in the house, saw Connie with her phone in her hand, raised as if to demand explanation or she'd call 911. The woman called out again, the harsh syllable reaching him on the breeze this time. "*Ry,*" she said, the little girl beginning to cry.

"*What?*" came the yell back from inside the house, DJ panting as he came up the walk.

"Go back to the car with Elise," Connie said.

"You go back to the car—what are you doing?"

"What am *I* doing? What is she," Connie started to say, but then the screen door slammed open and there was Ryan, same surfer-style shorts, but no shirt this time, his skin even more tan than before.

"Connie? Hey—how you doing? What's up?"

"*What's up?*" she said at the same time the woman said, "You know this bitch?"

Ryan winced. "David's wife—ex-wife. This is my girlfriend, Patrice."

"Quit crying now," Patrice said, jiggling the little girl.

"Is that Elise? Look at you, all grown up," Ryan said.

"Did I not tell you to stay in the car?" said Connie.

"What's going on?" said Elise, hugging her bad arm to her side.

Connie pulled her close. "That's what I wanna know. What are you doing here, *Ry?*" she added, giving the nickname a cold twist.

"Not so good to leave a house empty these days."

"So you just…" her hand floated up toward the house. "DJ, take Elise back to the car."

"*No*," said Elise, "I'm staying."

"Listen, Connie," said Ryan.

"No, you listen to me—"

"Now I see why he left," said Patrice.

"Shut up, Pats—you don't see anything. It's not like that," he said to Connie.

"What's it like, then?"

"*Connie*," said DJ, softly. "Let's just go."

"He invited me."

"*Invited*," said Patrice, the girl squirming in her arms.

"I'm not kidding, Patrice."

"*Ohh*, he's not kidding," she said, baby-talking to the girl.

Ryan took a step down toward her, then turned to Connie instead. "I would never do anything, you know … David said he wasn't," he glanced at Patrice. "He told me we—"

"No, no, no," Connie held up her hand. "Don't even tell me. Whatever the fuck—of course he did. My mistake."

"*Mom,*" said Elise.

"My mistake," Connie repeated, staring at the house. Then she took hold of Elise's free hand. "We're going."

"Nice to meet you," sneered Patrice.

"*Connie,*" Ryan called after her.

"C'mon, c'mon," Connie said, hustling them away. "I don't know what came over me. I saw that woman and I thought," she shook her head. "I don't know what I thought."

"You were pretty fierce there for a minute," said DJ.

"Oh, good God," she held out her hands, which were shaking.

"Who are those people?" said Elise. "Do I know that guy?"

"He must've seen you when you were little—but no. They're friends of your dad's."

"She didn't seem very friendly."

Connie let out a sharp laugh. "I never met that woman before—I thought she was a squatter. Doesn't matter," she said as they reached the car. "It's the bank's problem now. I'm sorry, Lise—you, too, Deej—I shouldn't have come this way. I shouldn't have stopped."

DJ thought of the last time he'd seen Ryan, of David banging his head against the steering wheel, his desperate wish to go fishing—a memory he'd just as soon overwrite. "You want to take a break? It's a beautiful day. We could drive to Brick Beach." He glanced toward his dresser, sticking out of the trunk. "No one's gonna steal that old thing."

"You know what? Let's do that."

"Really?"

"That okay with you, sweetie?"

At Connie's endearment, DJ gave Elise a sidelong glance, her chin ducking ever so slightly in response before she said, "Beach it is."

DJ held no fondness for his high school days, but he did miss that sense of promise. Not the kind people were always accusing him of not having lived up to, but the idea of your whole life still out there on the horizon. That was the feeling he'd always had at Brick Beach, ironic in its being the site of a ruin, doubly so as the punning destination where he and his high school cronies had often gone to get stoned, and tripled now by having sprung to mind in his hooky-playing association to David.

The expanse of parking lot and scrub grass, the bricks of the defunct Hutton Foundry cobbling the half-moon shore at low tide; the Hudson wide, the sky open, the low hills a buffer between you and the town as you looked out on the water; the faint rhythmic splash of shallow waves at your feet; all this had always added up to a solemn feeling of both solitude and freedom. A place where your voice would get lost on the wind, mare's tail clouds whipping across a sweep of crystalline blue. And what he remembered was just what they found. The air cool, the sun warm, the water sparkling.

Elise walked on ahead—her head bobbing, her hand weaving at her side, as though she were singing—and Connie fell in beside him.

"Just like you," she said.

"How's that?"

"A part of my life is over."

"Did we ever come here together?"

She shook her head.

"But you came here with your posse."

"My posse—yeah," she said, with a dismissive laugh. "We most certainly did."

As the distance between them and Elise widened, she turned with a skipping step, and waved.

"I used to think—I used to *feel* …" DJ looked at Connie, who waited for him to go on. "Like something would happen—like I'd get somewhere."

"And now here we are."

"Yeah—and now here we are. Brick Beach. Me with a dead wife—"

"Me with an ex-husband and an eleven-year-old daughter."

"We should write a country song."

"I loved that house," Connie said. "You think you know when something's over, but you really don't."

"Beginnings and endings," said DJ, and they let it rest at that.

After he'd turned in the key for the larger unit and they'd carried the last of his furniture downstairs, Elise sat down on one of the vinyl-seated chairs and said she was tired, asked if she couldn't just stay in the house by herself while they returned the Focus to Connie's colleague. DJ thought of David, upstairs for days on the living room couch. How after the accident Connie no longer trusted him to be in care of Elise for any amount of time, and it occurred to DJ that her reliance on *him* had been an act of faith.

"All I'm gonna be doing is reading," said Elise.

Connie looked from her to DJ. Making a don't-shoot-me face, he held up his hands, as if to say *you're gonna to have to do it sometime.*

"All right, all right. It's a brand-new day. I guess I give in."

"Hallelujah," said Elise, the back of her hand held mockingly to her forehead, as though she might faint.

"Don't make me sorry, now."

"*Connie Francis*," said DJ, and they both turned to him, Elise saying, "*Who?*" and Connie, "*What?*"

"Connie Francis—'Who's Sorry Now.'" He started singing the song.

Connie rolled her eyes at Elise and said, "I must've done something terrible in a past life."

With his clothes returned to their rightful dresser drawers, his salvaged furniture arranged, his treasured objects laid out on the Formica table, and in the far corner, Belinda's photos and negatives, safely stored in their plastic bins, DJ felt entitled to sleep as long as he could. Only the last box of her artwork was left to be unpacked. He'd even slid the coffee table forward and made up the convertible couch. But this tidy opening, this added room carved out of Connie's basement, with its newly cleared swath of cork floor, left him uneasy, as though it demanded something of him. Whereas the massive bulk of the ping-pong table, with his sister's bins and cartons stacked above and below, had formed a comforting barrier, a kind of seawall, that left him alone. This was the trouble with organizing, with cleaning up. It required maintenance, denounced the clutter that remained, and made space for all the emptiness to flood in.

When more sleep eluded him, DJ trudged upstairs, made fresh coffee and toast, determined to give the day a productive start. But after a smoke in the yard, the bushes and dark branches now awash with a budding green, he plunked himself down on the living room couch, sucked under an enormous wave of inertia.

Without the duty of picking up Elise, DJ had more time—just nothing he wanted to do with it. And without the convenience of Connie's car, he was disinclined to go into Kingston. Even the lure of Netflix didn't call out to him, and he'd left his iPad downstairs anyway, his phone on the kitchen table, beside his half-finished toast. That song by The Fugs floated into his mind, its droning and dirgelike listing of the days, each followed by the word *nothing*. Tuli Kupferberg, one of the originators of the band, had died at eighty-six, just the year before. But the remaining members, he'd seen in *The Voice*, were still set to perform in June at London's Meltdown Festival. DJ could play some guitar, work on his composition, but merely rested his chin on the back of Connie's sofa and looked out on the deserted street. Eighty-six. Good God. Would he live that long? Spend the next thirty years of his life in Hurley?

He'd meant to lay out a snack for Elise, to be waiting for her in the kitchen when she came through the door. But he must've dozed off, because he woke—still seated on the couch, his head flung back, his neck aching—to the sound of her clearing her throat. He sat up, rubbed his face.

Elise narrowed her eyes. "Were you having a nap?"

"One day you're going to see that taking a nap isn't necessarily a bad thing."

"And today?"

DJ cleared his own throat. "Today you're maybe a little bit right. *Mondays*," he said, with an exaggerated shudder. "How was yours? How was riding the bus?"

Elise shrugged. "Long. Slow. Boring."

"Did you make any friends?"

"On the *bus*?"

"I don't know—I just woke up."

"Clearly."

"Okay, okay," he said. "You win."

Elise sat down in the armchair and toed off her sneakers.

DJ yawned and stretched. "Should I whip us up some cookies?"

"As in open the box?"

"You want to make cookies? We could make cookies."

"I don't want to make cookies."

"No," he said, sinking back into the couch. "Neither do I."

Elise flapped her elbow in its sling. "Four more days." On Friday, Connie would leave work early to take her to the orthopedist. "I never told you how sorry—"

"*You did*," she cut him off. "Like a hundred times."

"Well, I'm glad someone's counting."

Elise snorted, just the way Connie would. "Cookies?" she asked, her offer now.

"You grab the box. I'll get the milk. Good for your bones."

She stuck out her tongue and made a gagging gesture.

DJ laughed. "I know the feeling." Maybe this, he thought, was what mattered—maybe this was the point. *And now you are, too*, Connie had said of his being a part of Elise's life. Maybe it was—maybe he wanted it to be true.

She got up and he followed her into the kitchen. A little company was the most he could offer her today. And if she still wanted, once her sling was off, he'd start teaching her to play guitar. It'd be something they could do together in the long string of afternoons.

For all his dreams of departure, his fantasies of other lives, he had not, in the end, been much for leaving. Out of all the places in the world that he might've gone—when he had the chance, when he had the money—he'd wound up back in Hurley. In time, Elise would be the one to leave, to embark on the life she would make her own. A life in which he'll have played only the tiniest of parts: a hazy, peripheral figure in memories mostly blotted out from this painful time of her parents' divorce. What did he have to pass on but a marbled glass egg and a few basic chords?

Do you play? some introverted boy hiding behind a guitar will ask her at a party years from now. *A little,* she'll say, waving him off with a laughing shake of her head. *When I was a kid, my uncle gave me a guitar.* And maybe she'll still have it—the Yamaha—leaning against a bookshelf, a beanbag chair, some hidden corner of her room.

The next day, DJ made a concerted effort. He got up in time to have his first coffee of the day with Connie and Elise. After they left, he took a shower, momentarily considered shaving off his beard, then chose to trim it instead, with a small scissors made to look like a stork that he'd noted in Connie's medicine chest. Embroidery scissors. Not a one of the women in his life embroidered, though most of them had owned a pair. His fingers barely fit through the delicate handles, but the blades were sharp enough to do the job and you couldn't help but admire their charm. Cutting his beard with an itty-bitty scissors was likely the last bit of goofy charm he himself had left, the chances of another big love—of any romantic connection in his life—grown slim. There was little he could do about that, except enjoy the clean sense of renewal his ablutions afforded.

He'd meant to settle downstairs at the Formica table, to return to his unfinished piece, but the day was too damn glorious. He tucked his cigarettes and his lighter into the pocket of a faded black denim jacket, picked up his phone and his keys, and headed for the stone houses on Main Street.

The one he favored had a grassy lane that led down one side to a small graveyard. The Old Hurley Burial Ground, now marked by a blue shield-shaped sign that replaced the one he recalled. White letters in a colonial-like font listed visiting hours as *Dawn to Dusk,* and DJ tried to imagine the eager tourist who would visit at daybreak to stand alone, as he was, among the leaning headstones. The names on some had been worn illegible by weather, the top layers of others sheered or slaking off, but those you could read were descendants of the original families who'd settled here. Grave rubbings were prohibited by the chipper sign, planted in the determined hopes of some heritage society to preserve what remained.

Medallions of pale green lichen dotted one round-cornered and rose-colored stone. He would have liked to lie down on the short stiff grass, to watch the series of comically puffy clouds slowly move across the bright blue sky, but the ground was too cold and damp. He ran his hand across the surface of that rough reddish stone, looked out through the tree trunks at the sloping field and low hills beyond, a view unchanged since he'd been a kid. It had never seemed spooky to come here. It was just a peaceful place.

The school bus did not come directly down Connie's street but dropped Elise and a younger girl where it curved into a broad intersection. DJ had been tempted to meet her there, to carry her heavy pack that last bit of her journey home, but didn't want to risk embarrassing her. Instead, he sat at the dining table, where he'd be sure to see her when she turned up the driveway—a reversal of their positions on his first evening back: Elise doing her homework beneath the halo of the Tiffany lamp; DJ outside in the brisk

March night, the glass egg tugging his coat to one side as he leaned into the incline.

At one end of the table, he'd set out a snack of mild salsa and chips, and at the other, the box of Belinda's artwork, the packing tape that had sealed it sliced through, but the flaps still unopened. As Elise trudged up the driveway, her jacket draped over her shoulders to accommodate the sling, he stood at the window, waving more and more wildly until she finally looked up. He grinned; the smile she returned indulgent as she shook her head, then raised her backpack slightly in lieu of the little stop-sign wave that was her signature greeting.

"Had your nap already?" she asked when they met at the kitchen door.

"No nap today. I know you've got homework, but I was hoping you might—"

"Think I could come in first?"

"Right—sorry. Let me take your pack."

"I got it."

"Can I hang up your jacket at least?"

The look she gave him was one of mocking suspicion. "Did you *break* something?"

"*No*." He took her jacket as she shrugged it off, hung it over one of the already laden hooks by the door. When he turned, she was still studying him.

"You're like the little kid who's knocked over the lamp."

"Not exactly what I was going for. Chips?" he said, gesturing toward the living room.

She followed him to the table. "*Aah*—the box of boxes. Okay, yeah—I'm in." She glanced down at the chips, then rubbed her fingers together. "Maybe some paper towels? I wouldn't want…"

"No," DJ said. "Me either."

Once they'd eaten their fill, he transferred their bowls over to the sideboard, then slid the box toward her. Elise opened the flaps, revealing a nest of plain newsprint and bubble-wrap. He would've liked to have her do the unpacking. But it was just too awkward for her with the sling, and she slid it back to him in another reversal—he the one grateful for her company now.

DJ took each item out without unwrapping it, moved the box to one of the empty chairs. In the bottom, there'd been a folder, and he opened that first, revealing a delicate line drawing, a portrait Belinda had done of him in pencil. It wasn't the best likeness, but she'd captured some essence of him, hunched over one of his guitars.

"No beard," said Elise. "When was that?"

Five years? Ten? He couldn't say. "Beard's recent. The drawing's much older."

There were a few watercolors and some oil pastels with buffering sheets of blank paper between them. Renderings of familiar objects. A teacup on the sill of their living room window with a crisscrossing of telephone lines and bare branches outside. A half-finished sketch of one of the red-vinyl-seated chairs now in Connie's basement. And one last pencil drawing. A startling self-portrait, before she'd lost her hair.

"*Oh*," said Elise. "That's her."

"Yeah," he said. Though the drawing had been smoothed and pressed flat in the box, it had been crumpled at some point—some private dark moment of Belinda's of which he'd been unaware. He closed the folder, reached for the largest of the newsprint-wrapped boxes. The rest were smaller; squares and narrow rectangles of the kind meant to hold jewelry. "Anyway. These are what I wanted to show you."

He carefully opened the layers of paper to reveal the cigar box that had topped the chifforobe, the tinted imagery of the fishermen beneath the glaze of varnish even more vibrant and poignant than he recalled.

"Oh, wow—can I see?"

DJ passed the box to Elise, who turned it this way and that, admiring each decorated side. She lifted the lid, revealing an interior collaged with fish of varying sizes, tinted the same subtle blues and greens.

"Oh, my God," he said. "I didn't remember that."

"It's beautiful. And funny." She set the box back on the table and readjusted her sling. "My dad liked to fish."

The smile he gave her was wistful, but all he could think to say was, "I know."

By the time Connie pulled into the driveway, Elise had finished her homework and was reading a book in the corner of the couch that everyone favored, the Yamaha still leaning unplayed against its upholstered arm. DJ had broken down the cardboard and wrapping materials and put them outside with the recycling; washed their dirty bowls, dried and put them away; and set the kitchen table for dinner. He'd left the folder of drawings on the sideboard, the gemlike boxes stacked on top, beside the record player—he wanted to show them to Connie, too.

Just as he'd met Elise, he went to greet her at the door, which he opened with a flourish and a bow.

"Oh, good," she said. "You can help me."

From her trunk, DJ lifted a white wicker hamper with a hinged lid. *Another box,* he thought, but what he said was, "Nice."

"It's neutral, anyway. Everything else was either huge or that hideous dark brown."

He carried the hamper downstairs, and when he came back up Connie was looking at the decoupaged boxes.

"These are kind of fantastic, aren't they? When did she make them?"

"A long time ago," he said, though he could've easily dated them to the year before his affair. Like the rest of his things, maybe it was time he just let that go.

"Can we put one on the mantel?" asked Elise.

"If he wants to. Deej?"

"Sure," he said. "You choose, E. Any one, except the cigar box. I'm gonna put that with the figurine."

"*Ah*," Connie said. "That reminds me. I got you something else." She went into the kitchen and came back with her bag. From a flat white box, then a thin foam pouch, DJ pulled out an elegant silver frame.

"For that photo of her—you don't want to just leave it leaning on the shelf like that."

DJ ran his finger along the smooth beveled edge. People had done so much for him lately—more than he deserved. But he couldn't think of the last time someone had given him an actual gift.

"You can always exchange it, if it's not—"

"No—I like it. It's perfect. Thank you."

"This one," said Elise.

The box she'd picked was a shallow square. An Audubon-like image of a magnolia blossom framed by deep green leaves covered its top, smaller scientific illustrations of other flowers and insects filling in the sides. The interior had a stained-glass-like surface of layered bits of colored tissue paper, and a curling yellow Post-it had been tucked inside for safekeeping. The sort of note he'd left Belinda countless times when he'd gone out for milk or cigarettes while she was still sleeping. Written inside the penned outline of a heart, the words *Back in 10*. Whatever he had or hadn't done with his life, however they'd helped or harmed each other—whoever Belinda had or hadn't really been—he'd loved her.

Though he'd stayed up late, DJ woke before dawn. He'd dreamt of David in the empty kitchen of the old house, a drywall trowel in his hand as he turned and grinned. The word *sprightly* came to mind, but the image left him with an anxious sadness that made his heart bang around his chest. As though he'd dreamt not about a man needlessly reframing the kitchen of a house he'd already lost, but of the last daring smile that David might flash him before he jumped off a bridge. DJ dismissed his darkly dreaming unconscious, rolled onto his back and held a hand to his sternum until the tightness subsided, but could find no peaceful reentry to sleep.

Daylight spilled down from the kitchen, slowly brightening the stairwell above his head, while the rest of the basement retained its soothing dimness, the shadowed fragments of his Brooklyn life—the celadon teapot, the curved metal corner of the Formica table—reflecting the faintest gleam of light.

DJ hummed the unresolved melody he'd been toying with for so long. The panning whoosh of a passing car he'd laid down beneath it was good, but he worried the mix was too simple, the composition too plain and uneventful overall. The yearning riff called out for a contrasting texture, some sharper, percussive edge to disturb the placid surface of the piece, the way the dream had rattled him into wakefulness. Or maybe that was merely a reminder of his own desire, his wish for something more. Belinda had died—she'd died—but he was still here.

He reached for his iPad, charging on his nightstand, returned once more to its rightful place beside his bed, such as—and regardless of where—it was. He could thread a heartbeat, or something like it, into the melody, but that was much too cornily on the nose. He would put in a bit of birdsong, those odd peeping chirps that announced the day, and he'd record the sounds of a weekday morning. The creak of footsteps overhead, the murmuring voices of his sister, his niece, the faint clattering of dishes—a subtle, domestic ambiance that would gently tinkle through. It didn't have to be harsh or big. The buzz of a neon filament, the clank of interlocking subway tracks that precedes a train—he would weave those in, too. A lush sampling of familiar sounds, the melody floating above it like a ribbon unspooling. A song of his days. That's what he would compose.

Acknowledgments

From my Warren Wilson days, special thanks to Megan Staffel, who saw the seed, and to Dominic Smith, who always believed I could if I wanted to. For mentorship and/or support, thanks also to Peter Turchi, Kevin McIlvoy, Lan Samantha Chang, Liam Callanan, Debra Spark, Debra Allbery, and Terri Leker.

Thanks to Tom Jenks for early encouragement of me as a writer, and to Jane Anne Staw, who saw me to the end of the first rough draft. Thanks to Peg Alford Pursell for championing my work and for the chance to read from an early draft at Studio 333. Thanks also to Will Allison and Olga Zilberbourg.

From my BookEnds fellowship year, thanks to my entire cohort, especially Daisy Florin, Céline Keating, and Jennifer Solheim; to Meg Wolitzer, who showed the way back in; to Amy Hempel for opening my eyes in ways large and small; and to Susie Merrell for more than I can say.

For bringing this book out into the world, thanks to Clay Reynolds, Kimberly Davis, Jacqueline Davis, and the rest of the Madville Publishing crew. Thanks also to everyone at Kaye Publicity: Julia Borcherts, Dana Kaye, Jordan Brown, and Nicole Leimbach.

Thanks to Marion Mell, who afforded me time and space across the years, and to Michael Mell and Kate Dayton for those two weeks in July that cracked the book open. To

Tracy Kirst for late-night texts and the trip upstate, and to Evelyn Burg for writing space and frank feedback. Thanks to Laurie Papell and Vanessa Stimac, who let me pick their brains on matters of social work and foreclosure. To John Bessler and Lydia Gould Bessler for the fantastic photos. Thanks to Tam Putnam for unending encouragement and support. And, as always, to Laura Lyons.

About the Author

Sue Mell is a writer from Queens, NY. She earned her MFA from Warren Wilson College and was a 2020 BookEnds fellow at SUNY Stony Brook Southampton. Her collection of micro essays, *Giving Care*, won the 2021 Chestnut Review Prose Chapbook Prize, and her collection of short stories, *A New Day*, was a finalist for the 2021 St. Lawrence Book Award. Other work has appeared in *Cleaver Magazine*, *Hippocampus Magazine*, *Jellyfish Review*, *Narrative Magazine*, and elsewhere.

Find her at suemellwrites.com and on Twitter @suemell2017